Frederic Harrison

The Choice of Books

Frederic Harrison

The Choice of Books

ISBN/EAN: 9783337426439

Printed in Europe, USA, Canada, Australia, Japan

Cover: Foto ©Andreas Hilbeck / pixelio.de

More available books at **www.hansebooks.com**

THE CHOICE OF BOOKS

BY

FREDERIC HARRISON

New York

MACMILLAN AND CO.

AND LONDON

1893

CHAPTER I.

HOW TO READ.

IT is the fashion for those who have any connection with letters to expatiate on the infinite blessings of literature, and the miraculous achievements of the press : to extol, as a gift above price, the taste for study and the love of reading. Far be it from me to gainsay the inestimable value of good books, or to discourage any man from reading the best ; but I often think that we forget that other side to this glorious view of literature—the misuse of books, the debilitating waste of brain in aimless, promiscuous, vapid reading, or even, it may be, in the

poisonous inhalation of mere literary
garbage and bad men's worst thoughts.

For what can a book be more than the
man who wrote it? The brightest genius
seldom puts the best of his own soul into
his printed page; and some famous men
have certainly put the worst of theirs.
Yet are all men desirable companions,
much less teachers, able to give us advice,
even of those who get reputation and
command a hearing? To put out of the
question that writing which is positively
bad, are we not, amidst the multiplicity
of books and of writers, in continual
danger of being drawn off by what is
stimulating rather than solid, by curiosity after something accidentally noto-
rious, by what has no intelligible thing
to recommend it, except that it is new?
Now, to stuff our minds with what is
simply trivial, simply curious, or that
which at best has but a low nutritive
power, this is to close our minds to what

is solid and enlarging, and spiritually sustaining. Whether our neglect of the great books comes from our not reading at all, or from an incorrigible habit of reading the little books, it ends in just the same thing. And that thing is ignorance of all the greater literature of the world. To neglect all the abiding parts of knowledge for the sake of the evanescent parts is really to know nothing worth knowing. It is in the end the same, whether we do not use our minds for serious study at all, or whether we exhaust them by an impotent voracity for desultory "information"—a thing as fruitful as whistling. Of the two evils I prefer the former. At least, in that case, the mind is healthy and open. It is not gorged and enfeebled by excess in that which cannot nourish, much less enlarge and beautify our nature.

But there is much more than this. Even to those who resolutely avoid the

idleness of reading what is trivial, a
difficulty is presented—a difficulty every
day increasing by virtue even of our
abundance of books.   What are the subjects, what are the class of books we are
to read, in what order, with what connection, to what ultimate use or object?
Even those who are resolved to read the
better books are embarrassed by a field of
choice practically boundless.   The longest
life, the greatest industry, joined to the
most powerful memory, would not suffice
to make us profit from a hundredth part
of the world of books before us.   If the
great Newton said that he seemed to
have been all his life gathering a few
shells on the shore, whilst a boundless
ocean of truth still lay beyond and unknown to him, how much more to each
of us must the sea of literature be a
pathless immensity beyond our powers
of vision or of reach—an immensity in
which industry itself is useless without

judgment, method, discipline ; where it is of infinite importance what we can learn and remember, and of utterly no importance what we may have once looked at or heard of. Alas! the most of our reading leaves as little mark even in our own education as the foam that gathers round the keel of a passing boat! For myself, I am inclined to think the most useful help to reading is to know what we should not read, what we can keep out from that small cleared spot in the overgrown jungle of "information," the corner which we can call our ordered patch of fruit-bearing knowledge. The incessant accumulation of fresh books must hinder any real knowledge of the old; for the multiplicity of volumes becomes a bar upon our use of any. In literature especially does it hold—that we cannot see the wood for the trees.

How shall we choose our books? Which are the best, the eternal, indispensable

books? To all to whom reading is something more than a refined idleness these
questions recur, bringing with them the
sense of bewilderment; and a still, small
voice within us is for ever crying out for
some guide across the Slough of Despond
of an illimitable and ever-swelling literature. How many a man stands beside
it, as uncertain of his pathway as the
Pilgrim, when he who dreamed the immortal dream heard him "break out
with a lamentable cry; saying, what
shall I do?"

And this, which comes home to all of
us at times, presses hardest upon those
who have lost the opportunity of systematic education, who have to educate
themselves, or who seek to guide the
education of their young people. Systematic reading is but little in favour
even amongst studious men; in a true
sense it is hardly possible for women.
A comprehensive course of home study,

and a guide to books, fit for the highest education of women, is yet a blank page remaining to be filled. Generations of men of culture have laboured to organise a system of reading and materials appropriate for the methodical education of men in academic lines. Teaching equal in mental calibre to any that is open to men in universities, yet modified for the needs of those who must study at home, remains in the dim pages of that melancholy volume entitled *Libri valde desiderati.*

I do not aspire to fill one of those blank pages ; but I long to speak a word or two, as the Pilgrim did to Neighbour Pliable, upon the glories that await those who will pass through the narrow wicket-gate. On this, if one can find anything useful to say, it may be chiefly from the memory of the waste labour and pitiful stumbling in the dark which fill up so much of the travail that one is fain to

call one's own education. We who have
wandered in the wastes so long, and lost
so much of our lives in our wandering,
may at least offer warnings to younger
wayfarers, as men who in thorny paths
have borne the heat and burden of the
day might give a clue to their journey to
those who have yet a morning and a
noon. As I look back and think of those
cataracts of printed stuff which honest
compositors set up, meaning, let us trust,
no harm, and which at least found them
in daily bread,—printed stuff which I
and the rest of us, to our infinitely small
profit, have consumed with our eyes, not
even making an honest living of it, but
much impairing our substance,—I could
almost reckon the printing press as
amongst the scourges of mankind. I am
grown a wiser and a sadder man, im-
portunate, like that Ancient Mariner, to
tell each blithe wedding guest the tale of
his shipwreck on the infinite sea of

printer's ink, as one escaped by mercy and grace from the region where there is water, water, everywhere, and not a drop to drink.

A man of power, who has got more from books than most of his contemporaries, once said : " Form a habit of reading, do not mind what you read ; the reading of better books will come when you have a habit of reading the inferior." We need not accept this *obiter dictum* of Lord Sherbrooke. A habit of reading idly debilitates and corrupts the mind for all wholesome reading ; the habit of reading wisely is one of the most difficult habits to acquire, needing strong resolution and infinite pains ; and reading for mere reading's sake, instead of for the sake of the good we gain from reading, is one of the worst and commonest and most unwholesome habits we have. And so our inimitable humourist has made delightful fun of the solid books,—which no gentleman's library should be without,—the Humes, Gibbons, Adam Smiths, which, he says, are not books at all, and prefers some "kind-hearted play-book," or at times the *Town and County Magazine*. Poor Lamb has not a little to answer for, in the revived relish for garbage unearthed from old theatrical dungheaps. Be it jest or earnest, I have little patience with the Elia-tic philosophy of the frivolous. Why do we still suffer the traditional hypocrisy about the dignity of literature—literature, I mean, in the gross, which includes about equal parts of what is useful and what is useless? Why are books as books, writers as writers, readers as readers, meritorious, apart from any good in them, or anything that we can get from them? Why do we pride ourselves on our powers of absorbing print, as our grandfathers did on their gifts in imbibing port, when we know that there is a mode of absorbing print, which makes it impossible that we can ever learn anything good out of books?

Our stately Milton said in a passage which is one of the watchwords of the English race, " as good almost kill a Man as kill a good Book." But has he not also said that he would "have a vigilant eye how Bookes demeane themselves, as well as men ; and do sharpest justice on them as malefactors"? . . . Yes ! they do kill the good book who deliver up their few and precious hours of reading to the trivial book ; they make it dead for them ; they do what lies in them to destroy " the precious life-blood of a master-spirit, imbalm'd and treasured up on purpose to a life beyond life ; " they " spill that season'd life of man preserv'd and stor'd up in Bookes." For in the wilderness of books most men, certainly all busy men, *must* strictly choose. If they saturate their minds with

the idler books, the " good book," which
Milton calls " an immortality rather than
a life," is dead to them : it is a book
sealed up and buried.

It is most right that in the great republic of letters there should be freedom
of intercourse and a spirit of equality.
Every reader who holds a book in his
hand is free of the inmost minds of men
past and present ; their lives both within
and without the pale of their uttered
thoughts are unveiled to him ; he needs
no introduction to the greatest ; he
stands on no ceremony with them ; he
may, if he be so minded, scribble " doggrel " on his Shelley, or he may kick
Lord Byron, if he please, into a corner.
He hears Burke perorate, and Johnson
dogmatise, and Scott tell his border tales,
and Wordsworth muse on the hillside,
without the leave of any man, or the
payment of any toll.   In the republic of
letters there are no privileged orders or

places reserved. Every man who has written a book, even the diligent Mr. Whitaker, is in one sense an author; '' a book's a book although there's nothing in't ;'' and every man who can decipher a penny journal is in one sense a reader. And your '' general reader,'' like the grave-digger in Hamlet, is hailfellow with all the mighty dead ; he pats the skull of the jester ; batters the cheek of lord, lady, or courtier ; and uses '' imperious Cæsar '' to teach boys the Latin declensions.

But this noble equality of all writers— of all writers and of all readers—has a perilous side to it. It is apt to make us indiscriminate in the books we read, and somewhat contemptuous of the mighty men of the past. Men who are most observant as to the friends they make, or the conversation they share, are carelessness itself as to the books to whom they intrust themselves, and the printed language with which they saturate their minds. Yet can any friendship or society be more important to us than that of the books which form so large a part of our minds and even of our characters? Do we in real life take any pleasant fellow to our homes and chat with some agreeable rascal by our firesides, we who will take up any pleasant fellow's printed memoirs, we who delight in the agreeable rascal when he is cut up into pages and bound in calf?

If any person given to reading were honestly to keep a register of all the printed stuff that he or she consumes in a year—all the idle tales of which the very names and the story are forgotten in a week, the bookmaker's prattle about nothing at so much a sheet, the fugitive trifling about silly things and empty people, the memoirs of the unmemorable, and lives of those who never really lived at all—of what a mountain of rubbish

would it be the catalogue !   Exercises for
the eye and the memory, as mechanical
as if we set ourselves to learn the names,
ages, and family histories of every one
who lives in our own street, the flirta-
tions of their maiden aunts, and the cir-
cumstances surrounding the birth of
their grandmother's first baby.

It is impossible to give any method to
our reading till we get nerve enough to
reject.   The most exclusive and careful
amongst us will (in literature) take boon
companions out of the street, as easily as
an idler in a tavern.   "I came across
such and such a book that I never heard
mentioned," says one, "and found it
curious, though entirely worthless."   "I
strayed on a volume by I know not
whom, on a subject for which I never
cared."   And so on.   There are curious
and worthless creatures enough in any
pot-house all day long ; and there is incessant talk in omnibus, train, or street

by we know not whom, about we care not what. Yet if a printer and a bookseller can be induced to make this gabble as immortal as print and publication can make it, then it straightway is literature, and in due time it becomes "curious."

I have no intention to moralise or to indulge in a homily against the reading of what is deliberately evil. There is not so much need for this now, and I am not discoursing on the whole duty of man. I take that part of our reading which by itself is no doubt harmless, entertaining, and even gently instructive. But of this enormous mass of literature how much deserves to be chosen out, to be preferred to all the great books of the world, to be set apart for those precious hours which are all that the most of us can give to solid reading ? The vast proportion of books are books that we shall never be able to read. A serious percentage of books are not worth reading at all. The really vital books for us we also know to be a very trifling portion of the whole. And yet we act as if every book were as good as any other, as if it were merely a question of order which we take up first, as if any book were good enough for us, and as if all were alike honourable, precious, and satisfying. Alas! books cannot be more than the men who write them; and as a fair proportion of the human race now write books, with motives and objects as various as human activity, books, as books, are entitled *à priori*, until their value is proved, to the same attention and respect as houses, steam-engines, pictures, fiddles, bonnets, and other products of human industry. In the shelves of those libraries which are our pride, libraries public or private, circulating or very stationary, are to be found those great books of the world *rari nantes in gurgite vasto*, those books

which are truly " the precious life-blood
of a master-spirit." But the very famil-
iarity which their mighty fame has bred
in us makes us indifferent ; we grow
weary of what every one is supposed to
have read ; and we take down something
which looks a little eccentric, some
worthless book, on the mere ground that
we never heard of it before.

Thus the difficulties of literature are
in their way as great as those of the
world, the obstacles to finding the right
friends are as great, the peril is as great
of being lost in a Babel of voices and an
ever-changing mass of beings. Books
are not wiser than men, the true books
are not easier to find than the true men,
the bad books or the vulgar books are
not less obtrusive and not less ubiquitous
than the bad or vulgar men are everywhere; the art of right reading is as long
and difficult to learn as the art of right
living. Those who are on good terms

with the first author they meet, run as much risk as men who surrender their time to the first passer in the street ; for to be open to every book is for the most part to gain as little as possible from any. A man aimlessly wandering about in a crowded city is of all men the most lonely ; so he who takes up only the books that he " comes across " is pretty certain to meet but few that are worth knowing.

Now this danger is one to which we are specially exposed in this age. Our high-pressure life of emergencies, our whirling industrial organisation or dis-organisation have brought us in this (as in most things) their peculiar difficulties and drawbacks. In almost everything vast opportunities and gigantic means of multiplying our products bring with them new perils and troubles which are often at first neglected. Our huge cities, where wealth is piled up and the requirements and appliances of life extended beyond the dreams of our forefathers, seem to breed in themselves new forms of squalor, disease, blights, or risks to life such as we are yet unable to master. So the enormous multiplicity of modern books is not altogether favourable to the knowing of the best. I listen with mixed satisfaction to the pæans that they chant over the works which issue from the press each day: how the books poured forth from Paternoster Row might in a few years be built into a pyramid that would fill the dome of St. Paul's. How in this mountain of literature am I to find the really useful book? How, when I have found it, and found its value, am I to get others to read it? How am I to keep my head clear in the torrent and din of works, all of which distract my attention, most of which promise me something, whilst so few fulfil that promise? The Nile is the source of the Egyptian's

bread, and without it he perishes of
hunger. But the Nile may be rather too
liberal in his flood, and then the Egyptian runs imminent risk of drowning.

And thus there never was a time, at
least during the last two hundred years,
when the difficulties in the way of making an efficient use of books were greater
than they are to-day, when the obstacles
were more real between readers and the
right books to read, when it was practically so troublesome to find out that
which it is of vital importance to know ;
and that not by the dearth, but by the
plethora of printed matter. For it comes
to nearly the same thing whether we are
actually debarred by physical impossibil-
ity from getting the right book into our
hand, or whether we are choked off from
the right book by the obtrusive crowd of
the wrong books ; so that it needs a strong
character and a resolute system of reading to keep the head cool in the storm

of literature around us. We read now-adays in the market-place—I would rather say in some large steam factory of letter-press, where damp sheets of new print whirl round us perpetually—if it be not rather some noisy book-fair where literary showmen tempt us with perform-ing dolls, and the gongs of rival booths are stunning our ears from morn till night. Contrast with this pandemonium of Leipsic and Paternoster Row the sub-lime picture of our Milton in his early retirement at Horton, when, musing over his coming flight to the epic heaven, practising his pinions, as he tells Diodati, he consumed five years of solitude in reading the ancient writers—

"Et totum rapiunt me, mea vita, libri."

Who now reads the ancient writers? Who systematically reads the great wri-ers, be they ancient or modern, whom the consent of ages has marked out as classics : typical, immortal, peculiar teachers of our race? Alas! the *Paradise Lost* is lost again to us beneath an inundation of graceful academic verse, sugary stanzas of ladylike prettiness, and ceaseless explanations in more or less readable prose of what John Milton meant or did not mean, or what he saw or did not see, who married his great-aunt, and why Adam or Satan is like that, or unlike the other. We read a perfect library about the *Paradise Lost*, but the *Paradise Lost* itself we do not read.

I am not presumptuous enough to assert that the larger part of modern literature is not worth reading in itself, that the prose is not readable, entertaining, one may say highly instructive. Nor do I pretend that the verses which we read so zealously in place of Milton's are not good verses. On the contrary,

I think them sweetly conceived, as musi-
cal and as graceful as the verse of any
age in our history. A great deal of our
modern literature is such that it is ex-
ceedingly difficult to resist it, and it is
undeniable that it gives us real information. It seems perhaps unreasonable to
many to assert that a decent readable
book which gives us actual instruction
can be otherwise than a useful com-
panion and a solid gain. Possibly
many people are ready to cry out upon
me as an obscurantist for venturing to
doubt a genial confidence in all literature
simply as such. But the question which
weighs upon me with such really crush-
ing urgency is this : What are the books
that in our little remnant of reading time
it is most vital for us to know ? For the
true use of books is of such sacred value
to us that to be simply entertained is to
cease to be taught, elevated, inspired by
books ; merely to gather information of

a chance kind is to close the mind to knowledge of the urgent kind.

Every book that we take up without a purpose is an opportunity lost of taking up a book with a purpose—every bit of stray information which we cram into our heads without any sense of its importance, is for the most part a bit of the most useful information driven out of our heads and choked off from our minds. It is so certain that information, *i.e.* the knowledge, the stored thoughts and observations of mankind, is now grown to proportions so utterly incalculable and prodigious, that even the learned whose lives are given to study can but pick up some crumbs that fall from the table of truth. They delve and tend but a plot in that vast and teeming kingdom, whilst those whom active life leaves with but a few cramped hours of study can hardly come to know the very vastness of the field before

them, or how infinitesimally small is the
corner they can traverse at the best.
We know all is not of equal value. We
know that books differ in value as much
as diamonds differ from the sand on the
seashore, as much as our living friend
differs from a dead rat. We know that
much in the myriad-peopled world of
books—very much in all kinds—is trivial,
enervating, inane, even noxious. And
thus, where we have infinite opportunities of wasting our efforts to no end, of
fatiguing our minds without enriching
them, of clogging the spirit without
satisfying it, there, I cannot but think,
the very infinity of opportunities is rob-
bing us of the actual power of using
them. And thus I come often, in my
less hopeful moods, to watch the re-
morseless cataract of daily literature
which thunders over the remnants of
the past, as if it were a fresh impedi-
ment to the men of our day in the way

of systematic knowledge and consistent powers of thought, as if it were destined one day to overwhelm the great inheritance of mankind in prose and verse.

I remember, when I was a very young man at college, that a youth, in no spirit of paradox, but out of plenary conviction, undertook to maintain before a body of serious students, the astounding proposition that the invention of printing had been one of the greatest misfortunes that had ever befallen mankind. He argued that exclusive reliance on printed matter had destroyed the higher method of oral teaching, the dissemination of thought by the spoken word to the attentive ear. He insisted that the formation of a vast literary class looking to the making of books as a means of making money, rather than as a social duty, had multiplied books for the sake of the writers rather than for the sake of the readers;

that the reliance on books as a cheap
and common resource had done much to
weaken the powers of memory ; that it
destroyed the craving for a general
culture of taste, and the need of artistic
expression in all the surroundings of
life. And he argued, lastly, that the
sudden multiplication of all kinds of
printed matter had been fatal to the
orderly arrangement of thought, and
had hindered a system of knowledge
and a scheme of education.

I am far from sharing this immature
view. Of course I hold the invention of
printing to have been one of the most
momentous facts in the whole history
of man. Without it universal social
progress, true democratic enlightenment,
and the education of the people would
have been impossible, or very slow, even
if the cultured few, as is likely, could
have advanced the knowledge of mankind without it. We place Gutemberg

amongst the small list of the unique and special benefactors of mankind, in the sacred choir of those whose work transformed the conditions of life, whose work, once done, could never be repeated. And no doubt the things which our ardent friend regarded as so fatal a disturbance of society were all inevitable and necessary, part of the great revolution of mind through which men grew out of the mediæval incompleteness to a richer conception of life and of the world.

Yet there is a sense in which this boyish anathema against printing may become true to us by our own fault. We may create for ourselves these very evils. For the art of printing has not been a gift wholly unmixed with evils ; it must be used wisely if it is to be a boon to man at all ; it entails on us heavy responsibilities, resolution to use it with judgment and self-control, and the will to resist its temptations and its perils.

Indeed, we may easily so act that we may make it a clog on the progress of the human mind, a real curse and not a boon. The power of flying at will through space would probably extinguish civilisation and society, for it would release us from the wholesome bondage of place and rest. The power of hearing every word that had ever been uttered on this planet would annihilate thought, as the power of knowing all recorded facts by the process of turning a handle would annihilate true science. Our human faculties and our mental forces are not enlarged simply by multiplying our materials of knowledge and our facilities for communication. Telephones, microphones, pantoscopes, steam-presses, and ubiquity-engines in general may, after all, leave the poor human brain panting and throbbing under the strain of its appliances, no bigger and no stronger than the brains of the men who heard Moses speak, and saw Aristotle and Archimedes pondering over a few worn rolls of crabbed manuscript. Until some new Gutemberg or Watt can invent a machine for magnifying the human mind, every fresh apparatus for multiplying its work is a fresh strain on the mind, a new realm for it to order and to rule.

And so, I say it most confidently, the first intellectual task of our age is rightly to order and make serviceable the vast realm of printed material which four centuries have swept across our path. To organise our knowledge, to systematise our reading, to save, out of the relentless cataract of ink, the immortal thoughts of the greatest—this is a necessity, unless the productive ingenuity of man is to lead us at last to a measureless and pathless chaos. To know anything that turns up is, in the infinity of knowledge, to know nothing. To read the first book we come across, in the wilderness of

books, is to learn nothing. To turn over
the pages of ten thousand volumes is to
be practically indifferent to all that is
good.

But this warns me that I am entering
on a subject which is far too big and
solemn. It is plain that to organise our
knowledge, even to systematise our reading, to make a working selection of books
for general study, really implies a complete scheme of education. A scheme of
education ultimately implies a system of
philosophy, a view of man's duty and
powers as a moral and social being—a
religion. Before a problem so great as
this, on which readers have such different
ideas and wants, and differ so profoundly
on the very premisses from which we
start, before such a problem as a general
theory of education, I prefer to pause. I
will keep silence even from good words.
I have chosen my own part, and adopted
my own teacher. But to ask men to

adopt the education of Auguste Comte, is almost to ask them to adopt Positivism itself.

Nor will I enlarge on the matter for thought, for foreboding, almost for despair, that is presented to us by the fact of our familiar literary ways and our recognised literary profession. That things infinitely trifling in themselves : men, events, societies, phenomena, in no way otherwise more valuable than the myriad other things which flit around us like the sparrows on the housetop, should be glorified, magnified, and perpetuated, set under a literary microscope and focussed in the blaze of a literary magic-lantern— not for what they are in themselves, but solely to amuse and excite the world by showing how it can be done—all this is to me so amazing, so heart-breaking, that I forbear now to treat it, as I cannot say all that I would.

The Choice of Books is really the choice

of our education, of a moral and intellectual ideal, of the whole duty of man. But though I shrink from any so high a theme, a few words are needed to indicate my general point of view in the matter.

In the first place, when we speak about books, let us avoid the extravagance of expecting too much from books, the pedant's habit of extolling books as synonymous with education. Books are no more education than laws are virtue ; and just as profligacy is easy within the strict limits of law, a boundless knowledge of books may be found with a narrow education. A man may be, as the poet saith, " deep vers'd in books, and shallow in himself." We need to know in order that we may feel rightly and act wisely. The thirst after truth itself may be pushed to a degree where indulgence enfeebles our sympathies and unnerves us in action. Of all men perhaps the book-lover needs most to be reminded that man's business here is to know for the sake of living, not to live for the sake of knowing.

A healthy mode of reading would follow the lines of a sound education. And the first canon of a sound education is to make it the instrument to perfect the whole nature and character. Its aims are comprehensive, not special ; they regard life as a whole, not mental curiosity; they have to give us, not so much materials, as capacities. So that, however moderate and limited the opportunity for education, in its way it should be always more or less symmetrical and balanced, appealing equally in turn to the three grand intellectual elements—imagination, memory, reflection : and so having something to give us in poetry, in history, in science, and in philosophy.

And thus our reading will be sadly

one-sided, however voluminous it be, if it entirely close to us any of the great types and ideals which the creative instinct of man has produced, if it shut out from us either the ancient world, or other European poetry, as important almost as our own. When our reading, however deep, runs wholly into "pockets," and exhausts itself in the literature of one age, one country, one type, then we may be sure that it is tending to narrow or deform our minds. And the more it leads us into curious byways and nurtures us into indifference for the beaten highways of the world, the sooner we shall end, if we be not specialists and students by profession, in ceasing to treat our books as the companions and solace of our lifetime, and in using them as the instruments of a refined sort of self-indulgence.

A wise education, and so judicious reading, should leave no great type of thought, no dominant phase of human nature, wholly a blank. Whether our reading be great or small, so far as it goes, it should be general. If our lives admit of but a short space for reading, all the more reason that, so far as may be, it should remind us of the vast expanse of human thought, and the wonderful variety of human nature. To read, and yet so to read, that we see nothing but a corner of literature, the loose fringe, or flats and wastes of letters, and by reading only deepen our natural belief that this island is the hub of the universe, and the nineteenth century the only age worth notice, all this is really to call in the aid of books to thicken and harden our untaught prejudices. Be it imagination, memory, or reflection that we address—that is, in poetry, history, science, or philosophy, our first duty is to aim at knowing something at least of the best, at getting some definite idea of the

mighty realm whose outer rim we are
permitted to approach.

But how are we to know the best ; how
are we to gain this definite idea of the
vast world of letters ? There are some
who appear to suppose that the "best"
are known only to experts in an esoteric
way, who may reveal to inquirers what
schoolboys and betting-men describe as
"tips." There are no "tips" in literature ; the "best" authors are never dark
horses ; we need no "crammers" and
"coaches" to thrust us into the presence
of the great writers of all time. "Crammers" will only lead us wrong. It is a
thing far easier and more common than
many imagine, to discover the best. It
needs no research, no learning, and is
only misguided by recondite information.
The world has long ago closed the great
assize of letters, and judged the first
places everywhere. In such a matter
the judgment of the world, guided and

informed by a long succession of accomplished critics, is almost unerring. When
some Zoilus finds blemishes in Homer,
and prefers, it may be, the work of some
Apollonius of his own discovering, we
only laugh. There may be doubts about
the third and the fourth rank ; but the
first and the second are hardly open to
discussion. The gates which lead to the
Elysian fields may slowly wheel back on
their adamantine hinges to admit now
and then some new and chosen modern.
But the company of the masters of those
who know, and in especial degree of the
great poets, is a roll long closed and
complete, and they who are of it hold
ever peaceful converse together.

Hence we may find it a useful maxim
that, if our reading be utterly closed to
the great poems of the world, there is
something amiss with our reading. If
you find Milton, Dante, Calderon, Goethe,
so much "Hebrew-Greek" to you; if

your Homer and Virgil, your Molière
and Scott, rest year after year undis-
turbed on their shelves beside your school
trigonometry and your old college text-
books ; if you have never opened the
Cid, the Nibelungen, Crusoe, and *Don
Quixote* since you were a boy, and are
wont to leave the Bible and the Imitation for some wet Sunday afternoon—
know, friend, that your reading can do
you little real good. Your mental di-
gestion is ruined or sadly out of order.
No doubt, to thousands of intelligent educated men who call themselves readers,
the reading through a Canto of *The Purgatorio,* or a Book of the *Paradise Lost,*
is a task as irksome as it would be to
decipher an ill-written manuscript in a
language that is almost forgotten. But,
although we are not to be always reading
epics, and are chiefly in the mood for
slighter things, to be absolutely unable
to read Milton or Dante with enjoyment,

is to be in a very bad way. Aristophanes,
Theocritus, Boccaccio, Cervantes, Molière
are often as light as the driven foam ;
but they are not light enough for the
general reader. Their humour is too
bright and lovely for the groundlings.
They are, alas ! "classics," somewhat
apart from our everyday ways ; they are
not banal enough for us ; and so for us
they slumber " unknown in a long night,"
just *because* they are immortal poets, and
are not scribblers of to-day.

When will men understand that the
reading of great books is a faculty to be
acquired, not a natural gift, at least not
to those who are spoiled by our current
education and habits of life ? *Ceci tuera
cela*, the last great poet might have said
of the first circulating library. An insatiable appetite for new novels makes it
as hard to read a masterpiece as it
seems to a Parisian boulevardier to live
in a quiet country. Until a man can

truly enjoy a draft of clear water bub-
bling from a mountain side, his taste is
in an unwholesome state. And so he
who finds the Heliconian spring insipid
should look to the state of his nerves.
Putting aside the iced air of the difficult
mountain tops of epic, tragedy, or psalm,
there are some simple pieces which may
serve as an unerring test of a healthy or
a vicious taste for imaginative work. If
the *Cid*, the *Vita Nuova*, the *Canter-
bury Tales*, Shakespeare's *Sonnets*, and
Lycidas pall on a man ; if he care not
for Malory's *Morte d'Arthur* and the
Red Cross Knight; if he thinks *Crusoe*
and the *Vicar* books for the young ; if he
thrill not with *The Ode to the West
Wind*, and *The Ode to a Grecian Urn;*
if he have no stomach for *Christabel* or
the lines written on *The Wye above Tin-
tern Abbey*, he should fall on his knees
and pray for a cleanlier and quieter
spirit.

The intellectual system of most of us in these days needs "to purge and to live cleanly." Only by a course of treatment shall we bring our minds to feel at peace with the grand pure works of the world. Something we ought all to know of the masterpieces of antiquity, and of the other nations of Europe. To understand a great national poet, such as Dante, Calderon, Corneille, or Goethe, is to know other types of human civilisation in ways which a library of histories does not sufficiently teach. The great masterpieces of the world are thus, quite apart from the charm and solace they give us, the master instruments of a solid education.

CHAPTER II.

POETS OF THE OLD WORLD.

I PASS from all systems of education—
from thought of social duty, from meditation on the profession of letters—to
more general aud lighter topics. I will
deal now only with the easier side of
reading, with matter on which there is
some common agreement in the world.
I am very far from meaning that our
whole time spent with books is to be
given to study. Far from it. I put the
poetic and emotional side of literature
as the most needed for daily use. I take
the books that seek to rouse the imagination, to stir up feeling, touch the heart
—the books of art, of fancy, of ideals,
such as reflect the delight and aroma of
life. And here how does the trivial,

provided it is the new, that which stares at us in the advertising columns of the day, crowd out the immortal poetry and pathos of the human race, vitiating our taste for those exquisite pieces which are a household word, and weakening our mental relish for the eternal works of genius! Old Homer is the very fountain-head of pure poetic enjoyment, of all that is spontaneous, simple, native, and dignified in life. He takes us into the ambrosial world of heroes, of human vigour, of purity, of grace. He is the eternal type of the poet. In him, alone of the poets, a national life is transfigured, wholly beautiful, complete, and happy: where care, doubt, decay are as yet unborn. Here is the secular Eden of the natural man—man not yet fallen or ashamed. All later poetry paints an ideal world, conceived by a sustained effort of invention. Homer paints a world which he saw.

Most men and women can say that
they have read Homer, just as most of
us can say that we have studied Johnson's Dictionary. But how few of us
take him up, time after time, with fresh
delight! How few have even read the
entire Iliad and Odyssey through!
Whether in the resounding lines of the
old Greek, as fresh and ever-stirring as
the waves that tumble on the seashore,
filling the soul with satisfying silent
wonder at its restless unison ; whether in
the quaint lines of Chapman, or the
clarion couplets of Pope, or the closer
versions of Cowper, Lord Derby, of
Philip Worsley, or in the new prose version, Homer is always fresh and rich.*

---

* Homer has exercised a greater variety
of translators than any other author whatever. Of them all I prefer Lord Derby's
Iliad, and Philip Worsley's Odyssey.
Children usually begin their Homer through

And yet how seldom does one find a friend spellbound over the Greek Bible of antiquity, whilst they wade through torrents of magazine quotations from a petty versifier of to-day, and in an idle vacation will graze, as contentedly as cattle in a fresh meadow, through the

---

Pope, which has certainly the ring and fire of a poem, though it is not Homer's. Lord Derby preserves something of the *dignity* of the Iliad, which is essential to it; and Worsley preserves much of the fairy-tale charm of the Odyssey. His Iliad, completed by Conington, is almost a mistake. Chapman, poet as he is, is rather archaic for ordinary readers, and too loose for scholarly readers. Cowper is rather monotonous. The rest are rather experiments than results. To English hexameters there are euphonic obstacles which seem to be insuperable. The first line of the Iliad has thirty letters, of which twelve

chopped straw of a circulating library.
A generation which will listen to *Pina-
fore* for three hundred nights, and will
read M. Zola's seventeenth romance,
can no more read Homer than it could
read a cuneiform inscription. It will read
about Homer just as it will read about a

---

only are consonants. The first line of
Evangeline has fifty-four letters, of which
thirty-six are consonants. Thus, whilst a
Greek in pronouncing his hexameter has
twelve hard sounds to form, the English-
man has thirty-six, or exactly three times
as many.

Of the prose translations, that of Mr.
Andrew Lang and his friends is as perfect
as prose translation of verse can be. It
necessarily loses the movement, the lilt,
and the subtle charm of the verse. Flaxman's designs will be of great help in en-
joying Homer, and also what E. Coleridge,
Grote, Gladstone, M. Arnold, and Symonds
have written.

cuneiform inscription, and will crowd to see a few pots which probably came from the neighbourhood of Troy. But to Homer and the primeval type of heroic man in his simple joyousness the cultured generation is really dead, as completely as some spoiled beauty of the ballroom is blind to the bloom of the heather or the waving of the daffodils in a glade.

It is a true psychological problem, this nausea which idle culture seems to produce for all that is manly and pure in heroic poetry. One knows—at least every schoolboy has known—that a passage of Homer, rolling along in the hexameter or trumpeted out by Pope, will give one a hot glow of pleasure and raise a finer throb in the pulse ; one knows that Homer is the easiest, most artless, most diverting of all poets ; that the fiftieth reading rouses the spirit even more than the first—and yet we find ourselves

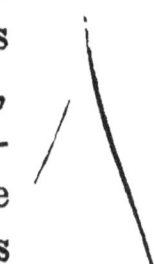

(we are all alike) painfully pshawing
over some new and uncut barley-sugar
in rhyme, which a man in the street
asked us if we had read, or it may be
some learned lucubration about the site
of Troy by some one we chanced to meet
at dinner.   It is an unwritten chapter in
the history of the human mind, how this
literary prurience after new print un-
mans us for the enjoyment of the old
songs chanted forth in the sunrise of
human imagination.   To ask a man or
woman who spends half a lifetime in
sucking magazines and new poems to
read a book of Homer, would be like
asking a butcher's boy to whistle "Ade-
laida."   The noises and sights and talk,
the whirl and volatility of life around
us, are too strong for us.   A society
which is for ever gossiping in a sort of
perpetual "drum" loses the very faculty
of caring for anything but "early copies"
and the last tale out.   Thus, like the

tares in the noble parable of the Sower,
a perpetual chatter about books chokes
the seed which is sown in the greatest
books of the world.

I speak of Homer, but fifty other great
poets and creators of eternal beauty
would serve my argument. What Homer
is to epic, that is Æschylus to the tragic
art—the first immortal type. In majesty
and mass of pathos the Agamemnon remains still without a rival in tragedy.
The universality and inexhaustible versatility of our own Shakespeare are unique
in all literature. But the very richness
of his qualities detracts from the symmetry and directness of the dramatic impression. For this reason neither is Lear,
nor Othello, nor Macbeth, nor Hamlet
(each supreme as an imaginative creation) so typically perfect a tragedy as
the Agamemnon. In each of the four
there are slight incidents which we could
spare without any evident loss. The

Agamemnon alone of tragedies has the
absolute perfection of a statue by Pheidias.   The intense *crescendo* of the catastrophe, the absolute concentration of
interest, the statuesque unity of the
grouping, the mysterious halo of religion
with which the ancient legend sanctified
the drama, are qualities denied to any
modern.[1]

---

[1] Of all the translations of the Agamemnon, I prefer that of Mr. E. D. A. Morshead, which seems to me by its union of
accurate version with poetic vigour to stand
in the front rank of English verse translation.   Milman's version is the work of a
poet, but not so completely master of the
Greek ; Mr. R. Browning's is also the work
of a poet and a scholar, but its uncouth-
ness is not the rugged majesty of Æschylus.   The Agamemnon is at times stormy
in diction ; it is never queer.   Miss Swanwick's beautiful translation has been published with Flaxman's designs.   If Flax-

If the seven surviving dramas of Æschylus had followed into black night the other sixty-three, which we have lost, we should probably regard Œdipus the King of Sophocles as the type of the pure drama. And, in the exquisite tenderness and nobility of soul of the Antigone and the Œdipus at Colonus, Sophocles reaches a note of pathos, wherein Æschylus himself had inferior, and Shakespeare alone an equal mastery.[1] So, too, in comedy, Aristophanes is the

---

man's genius is not so much in harmony with Æschylus as with Homer, he is quite at his best in the Agamemnon.

[1] Mr. E. D. A. Morshead has been as successful with the Œdipus King of Sophocles as with the Trilogy of Æschylus. Professor Lewis Campbell's translation of Sophocles is most elegant and, with the accuracy of a scholar, gives us something of the grace and lyric charm of Sophocles.

eternal type. Inexhaustible fancy, the wildest humour, the keenest wit, the subtlest eye for character, combine in him with perennial inventiveness and exquisite melody. Demagogy, Presumption, Pedantry, every phase of extravagance and affectation, pass in turns across a stage which reaches from boisterous farce to splendid lyric poetry. The Phallic license of this ungovernable jester—a license without limit and, in familiar literature, without a match, is less a matter of vice or obscenity, than of social, local, and even religious convention.[1]

---

[1] It is singular that of this poet, in many respects the most Shakespearean of all the ancients, some of the best translations exist. Together they undoubtedly enable us to enter into the true Aristophanic spirit. The free version of Hookham Frere is almost as good as any translation in verse

Greece gave us the model and eternal type of written language, not only in epic, tragic, and comic poetry, but in imaginative prose, and in pure lyric. We come upon those marvellous fragments of Alcman, Alcæus, Sappho, and Tyrtæus, rescued for us by the diligent love of scholars, with the same sense of acute regret that we first see some head, trunk, or limb of the golden age of Greek sculpture unearthed from beneath a pile

---

of an untranslatable ancient can be. Those of Cumberland and T. Mitchell have spirit, and the recent versions by B. B. Rogers have accuracy as well as spirit. Altogether we have an adequate rendering of some eight or nine of these masterpieces. One who will read the commentaries of Mitchell, Frere, Rogers, and the illustrations given us by Symonds and Mahaffy will get a living idea of this, the older comedy, the most amazing avatar of the pure Attic genius.

of rubbish. The history of mankind records few such irreparable losses as the lyrics of Greece, of which almost every line that is saved seems a faultless gem of art. It gives us a striking impression of the poetic fertility of Greece, when we remember that, from Homer to Longus, we have at least thirteen centuries of almost unbroken productiveness. No other literature has any continuous record so vast, nor any other language such an unbroken life.[1] Here, as

---

[1] Of Pindar and Theocritus we now possess prose versions, as perfect, I believe, as any prose version of a poet can be. Mr. E. Myers' recent translation of Pindar, and Mr. Lang's translation of Theocritus, Bion, and Moschus, preserve for us something even of the form of the original. I am wont to look on Mr. Lang's Theocritus, in particular, as a *tour-de-force* in translation at present without a rival. He has caught,

elsewhere and so often, Mr. Symonds is an unerring guide ; and they who will study with care his versions and illustrations may at least come to know how great is our loss in the disappearance of the

---

although using prose, the music and lilt of the Greek verse. His version of the Pharmaceutria, of the Epithalamium, of the Adonis, suggests a metrical melody as plainly as does the English version of the Psalms. The excellent translation in verse by Mr. C. S. Calverley does not retain the music at all. Nor can I read patiently the verse translations of Pindar. There is no complete English version of the Poetæ Lyrici of Greece ; but there are translations of some beautiful Fragments by Frere, Dean Milman, Lord Derby, J. A. Symonds, father and son, Professor Conington, and many others. Those of Milman can almost be read as poetry. The immortal Fragments of Sappho have exercised the art of a long line of translators from Catullus

works of which these are but the remnant and the fragments. One of the
most perfect of all translations is the
quaint version of the Daphnis and Chloe
of Longus, by old Amyot, improved by
P. L. Courier. It is amongst the prob-

to Rossetti and Mr. Symonds—all, alas !
in vain. The greatest recorded genius
amongst women has left us those dazzling
lines, which of all human poetry have
been the most intensely searched, the most
fondly remembered. But they remain essentially Greek ; no other tongue can tell
their fiery tale.

Chapman has given us Hesiod as well as
Homer, and Marlowe and Chapman a vari-
ation on Musæus. Frere has attempted to
recall Theognis to life. But the metrical
versions of these Greek lyrics, the most
exquisitely artless, and yet the most magi-
cally graceful in the world, are little more,
at the best, than scholarly exercises of a
learned leisure.

lems of history that this most Pagan,
most Hellenic, and most romantic of
pastorals, was contemporary with the
" City of God ; " was composed at a time
when Christianity had long been the
official religion of Greece, when Chris-
tendom was torn into segments by rival
heresies and sects, and when the warlike
barbarians of the North had already
plunged into chaos large portions of the
Empire. The Hellenic genius of beauty,
after twelve centuries of incessant energy, may be heard in this, its last song ;
unheeding revolutions and battles alike
in thought, in society, and in life.

Passing from Greece to Italy, there
is a great poetic void. There is no Roman Homer. Such Iliad as Rome has,
must be sought for in Livy. The legends
and lays which he built into the founda-
tions of his resplendent story remain still
traceable, just as, on the Capitol hill to
this day, we see masses of peperino and

red tufa, where the Tabularium serves
as basement to the Renaissance Palace
which Michael Angelo raised for the
Senator. That great imperial race did
not embody its life as a whole in any
national poem. The Æneid of Virgil
was the almost academic equivalent of a
national epic. It bears to the Iliad some
such relation as the *Polyeucte* of Cor-
néille bears to the Agamemnon of
Æschylus. Yet so touching are its episodes, so heroic its plan and conception,
so consummate the form, so profound
its influence over later generations of
men, that it must for ever hold a place
in the eternal poetry of mankind.[1]

---

[1] The translation of Virgil is a problem
even more perplexing than that of Homer.
Glorious John treated his epic with even
less regard for the original than Pope, and
with far less grace and dignity. The
Æneid is hardly tolerable in the racy

The other poetry of Rome is chiefly
didactic, moral, or social. Rome has no
tragedy except in her history, no comedy
that is not more than half Greek. Horace, Ovid, Catullus, we read for their
inimitable witchery of phrase ; Juvenal,
Plautus, and Terence, we read for their
insight into men ; Lucretius for his wonderful force of meditation, so strangely
in anticipation of modern thought. But

---

couplets which give point to Absalom
and Achitophel. Mr. Conington's attempt
to turn the Æneid into the rhyme of Mar-
mion is a sad waste of ingenuity ; nor does
Mr. Morris mend matters by turning it into
a "marry-come-up," "my merry men all"
kind of ballad. The majesty, the distinc-
tion, the symmetry of Virgil evaporate in
both ; more than in Dryden, who, at any
rate, was a master of the English language
and of the rhymed couplet. Mr. Conington's excellent prose version does not re-

the genius of Roman poetry is wrapt up in its form. It is hardly communicable at all except in the original words. Translations of it are vain exercises of ingenuity.

Horace remains to this day the type of the untranslatable. Such wit, grace, sense, fire, and affection never took such perfect form—the perfect form of some gem of Athens, or some coin of Syracuse

---

tain, hardly seeks to retain, any echo of the music, any trace of the mien of the mighty Roman. It is useful to those who need help in reading Virgil, but it is not such a veritable version as Mr. Lang has given us of Homer and Theocritus, and Dr. Carlyle of the Inferno, or Amyot of Daphnis and Chloe. There is but one way in which what used to be called the "English reader" can enjoy his Virgil, and that way is to learn Latin enough to read him, and I earnestly counsel him so to do.

— save in those irrecoverable lyrics, where Sappho and Alcæus, they tell us, clothed yet richer thoughts in even rarer words.[1]

---

[1] Since Horace, by common consent, is untranslatable, the translations of him, as might be expected, are innumerable. Where Milton and Pope did not succeed, and where many a poet has failed, the prize is not within the reach of mortal man. Lord Derby's shots, perhaps of all, come nearest the bull's-eye. Some odes of Mr. Conington are readable; he succeeds far better with Horace than with Virgil. On the whole, perhaps, the English reader, who will study the commentary and version of Sir Theodore Martin, will get some definite idea of one of the most interesting figures in the whole range of letters, of the most modern and most familiar of the ancients.

Mr. Munro and Mr. Robinson Ellis have given us editions of Lucretius and of Ca-

It is a melancholy thought that, with all our new apparatus of scholarship and antiquarian research, the present generation has less vital hold on ancient poetry than our forefathers had. We

tullus which are an honour to English scholarship. The admirable prose version of Lucretius by Mr. Munro is chiefly of service to the student. The poetic power of the great philosopher-poet is seen only in skeleton. Mr. Ellis' crabbed verse translation of Catullus is mainly useful as a specimen of what a translation should not be. Scholars have an incurable way with them, of pelting us with queer uncommon phrases which have a meaning perhaps identical with the original words, but which together produce a grotesque effect, wholly out of harmony with the poem translated. How can lines such as—

" Late-won loosener of the wary girdle,"

or—

" Pray unbody him only nose for ever,"

read it less, quote it less, care for it less than of old. The pedantry of collators and grammarians, the mechanic routine of the examination system, have almost quenched that noble zest in the classics

---

represent the airy notes of the most fantastic of the Latin poets, pouring forth his song like the lark on the wing? Or, again, can such a line as—

"The race is to Ate glued,"

represent the majestic terror of Æschylus?

In spite of Marlowe, Pope, Dryden, and Rowe, who have all tried their hands on the Latin poets, it may be doubted if any translation of them in verse can give any part of their genius, unless it be of the Satires and the Comedies, of which spirited and readable versions, or rather paraphrases, exist. But better than translations are such admirable commentaries on the classics, as those of Sellar, Symonds, F. Myers, Simcox, Theodore Martin, Conington, Ellis, and Munro.

which was meat and drink to them of old, to Fox, Johnson, Addison, or Milton. Our boys at university and school are ground between the upper and the nether millstone of interminable "passes," "Little-goes," and "Finals;" so that to a prize boy at Eton or Baliol his classical authors are no longer a glorious field of enjoyment and of thought—but what a cricket-ground is to a professional bowler, a monotonous hunting-ground for a good "average" and gate-money.

A rational choice of books would restore to us the healthy use of the great classics of antiquity. Most of us find that true sympathy with our classics begins only then, when our academic study of them is wholly at an end. The college prizeman and the college tutor cannot read a chorus in the Trilogy but what his mind instinctively wanders on optatives, choriambi, and that happy conjecture of Smelfungus in the antistrophe. A less constant thumbing of glossaries and commentaries is needful to those who would enjoy.

But even to those to whom the originals are quite or almost closed, a conception of the ancient authors is an indispensable condition of rational education. A clear idea of their subjects, methods, form, and genius, is within the power of all systematic readers. Our own generation has multiplied the resources by which they may be made familiar. All such resources have their value ; a combination of them can give us something, though all together cannot give us the whole. A curious profusion of translation, in prose and in verse, singular critical insight, and unwearied zeal to present antiquity to us as a whole, is the special service of our own age. Painting, poetry, music, the stage, are all working to the same end. So that, with all that art, criti-

cism, and translation can do, the un-
learned, if they seek it diligently, may
find the entrance, at least, into the
portico of Athene.

It is the age of accurate translation.
The present generation has produced a
complete library of versions of the great
classics, chiefly in prose, partly in verse,
more faithful, true, and scholarly than
anything ever produced before. It is
the photographic age of translation ;
and all that the art of sun-pictures has
done for the recording of ancient build-
ings, and more than that, the art of
literal translation has done for the understanding of ancient poetry. A complete translation of a great poem is, of
course, an impossible thing. The finest
translation is at best but a copy of a
part ; it gives us more or less crudely
some element of the original ; the colour,
the light and shade, the glow, are not
there, lost as completely as they are in

a photograph. But in the large photograph—say of the Sistine Madonna—the
lines and the composition arc there, as
no human hand ever drew them. And
so, in a fine translation, the thought
survives. One method gives us one element, another method some fresh element, and together we may get some
real impression of the mighty whole.

Now, when some of us may have
partly lost touch of the original, and
some may never have acquired it, the
use of translations, especially the use of
varied translations, may give us much.
In the very front rank come, for verse,
Morshead's *Trilogy* of Æschylus, and
his *Œdipus the King* of Sophocles, Mr.
Philip Worsley's *Odyssey*, Lord Derby's
Iliad, Frere's *Aristophanes*, the *Greek
Lyrics* of Milman, and Fitzgerald's *Calderon*. These are all readable as poems
in themselves ; but they hardly come up
to the typical examples of translations—

translations of a poet by a poet—such
as Shelley's Fragments, and Coleridge's
Wallenstein. It is greatly to be deplored
that Coleridge did not act on Shelley's
suggestion and translate *Faust*. They
who conscientiously struggle through
Hayward, Sir Theodore Martin, Miss
Swanwick, Bayard Taylor, and the rest,
would have been grateful to see *Faust*,
in the language of *Wallenstein*, *Kubla
Khan*, and *Christabelle*. But there is
only one of the translators of our day
whom we can read without the continual
sense that we are reading a translation.
Edward Fitzgerald's translations alone
read as if they were original composi-
tions; but the question for ever recurs,
Are they translations at all?

For prose we can hardly have anything
better than the *Homer* by Mr. Andrew
Lang, Professor Butcher, E. Myers, and
Walter Leaf; Mr. Lang's *Theocritus;*
Mr. Myers' *Pindar;* Mr. Conington's

prose *Virgil;* Munro's *Lucretius;* the *Inferno,* by John Carlyle ; *Dante,* by Lamennais ; the *Cid,* by Damas Hinard. Each of these, in its own way, gives us almost as much as translation ever can give. The prose translator naturally fails to give us music, movement, form ; but he gives us the substantial thought with almost complete fulness. The verse translation, in the hands of a poet, if it somewhat miss the thought, recalls to us some echoes of the lilt of the poem. Put the two together, use them as helps alternately, and much of the real comes forth to us. Take the prose *Iliad* of Leaf, Lang, and E. Myers, and then with that listen to the music of old Chapman, and the martial ring of some battle-piece in Pope or Lord Derby, and something more than an echo of Homer is ours. Or, what is better still, take the prose *Odyssey* of Butcher and Lang, and therewith read the exquisite verse of Philip Worsley, and some of the quiet pieces of Cowper, and then with the designs of Flaxman, and the local colour of Wordsworth's Greece, and Mahaffy and Symonds, the imagination can restore us a vision of the Ithacan tale. The *Inferno* of John Carlyle has an even greater advantage; for the Biblical style, by association, suggests the music and pathos of the poetry, and that without the affectation which attends all reproductions of Biblical phraseology. It is continued by A. J. Butler in the *Purgatory* and *Paradise*. The archaic French of Lamennais' version has much the same effect. These with Cary, and the beautiful book of Dean Church, ought to enable us to get at the sense and something of the form of the Divine Comedy.

With all this wealth of translation we have such elaborate general works on the history of ancient literature as those of K. O. Muller, Mure, and Simcox; and the fine studies of Greek and Latin poets, by J. A. Symonds, F. Myers, Professors Munro, Robinson Ellis, Conington, and Sellar ; and by Mr. Gladstone, and Matthew Arnold. With all this abundance of critical resource, one who knows anything of Latin and Greek can learn to enjoy his ancient poets ; and even one who knows nothing can gain some idea of their genius.

What Homer is to Greece, the early national epics and myths of other countries are to them ; far inferior to the Greek in beauty, of less perennial value, but the true germ of the literature of each. Yet to the bulk of readers this fountain-head of all poetry lies in a region unexplored, as unknown as to our fathers were the sources of the Nile— *fontium qui celat origines.* The early poetry of India, with its wonderful mythology, rich as it is for its own poetic worth, opens to us more of the old Oriental mind than many a history. Sir William Jones, who first made this poetry accessible to Europe, was, in the intellectual world, the Columbus who joined two continents. Since his day the labours of Professors Wilson, Max Müller, and Monier Williams have opened to us a new region of poetry, united two twin brethren, who have long lived estranged. Such a book as the Arabian Nights we are too apt to look on as a story-book, even perhaps a story-book for children. It is not so. Read between the lines, it presents to us the mind and civilisation of Islam, the civil side of that of which the Koran is the religious.

There is the same epical embodiment of the national genius in our early European poetry. The fierce Teuton and Norse races have each left us their own myths, of which this century alone has recognised the wild and tragic power, and has, in so many forms, now opened to the modern reader. The highest note of the barbaric drama is reached in the Nibelungen Lied—the Thyestean tragedy of the North—which, but for the excessive appeal to horror in its weird imagery, might take its place with the great epics of the world. Nay, that last terrific scene in the Hall of Etzel rests for ever on the memory as hardly inferior to that other supreme hour of vengeance, when the rags fall from off Odysseus, and he confronts the suitors with his awful bow.[1]

---

[1] Although every one, since Carlyle gave his sketch of it (*Miscell.* vol. iii.), has known something of the Nibelungen Lied, and although modern poetry and art have made it, in one form or other, as familiar as any legendary poem extant, it is singular that we have not got it in English in any satisfactory shape. For my part I prefer

France, too, has her epic literature in the *Chansons de Gestes*, the *Romans*, the *Fabliaux*—especially in the *Chanson de Roland*, and the *Roman du Renart*, which should serve as types of the rest. Spain and the Celtic race of Western England and Western France have two

---

the German to the Norse type of the epic; for the latter has nothing equivalent to the sustained and elaborate drama of the vengeance of Chriemhild. But where we can see plainly the scheme and bones of a mighty poem, it is vexatious to read it spun out into the monotonous garrulity of the existing 2459 stanzas, or to read it in the halting, stammering doggrel of Lettsom. We need much a somewhat condensed version of the Siegfried and Chriemhild myth in the plain and stirring English in which Southey cast the Cid, or, better still, in that wherein Malory cast the old Arthurian Chansons.

great epic cycles, which cluster round the
names of the Cid and of Arthur.

Whilst the Spanish Cycle is the more
national, heroic, and stirring, the Arthurian Cycle is the best embodiment of
chivalry, of romance, of gallantry. The
vast cluster of tales which envelop King
Arthur and his comrades is the expression of European chivalry and the feudal
genius as a whole, idealising the knight,
the squire, the lady, the princess of the
Middle Ages. For all practical purposes,
we English have it in its best form ; for
the compilation of Sir Thomas Malory
is wrought into a mould of pure English,
hardly second to the English of the
Bible.[1] And yet our Arthurian Cycle
has left far less traces on our national
character than the cycle of the Cid has

---

[1] It will be seen that in the original text
of Malory about 98 per cent of the words
are pure English, without Latin alloy.

left on that of Spain. How high and loyal a type is each! Of the Cid it is said—

"Lo que non ferie el Caboso por quanto en
    el mundo ha ;
Una deslealtanza, ca non la fizo algu-
    andre."

"That which the Perfect One would not
    do for all that the world holds ;
For a deed of disloyalty he never yet
    did in aught." [1]

---

[1] The Cid Cycle of poems has fared better than the Nibelungen. Besides the well-known translations by Lockhart in verse, and by Southey in prose, there is a stirring fragment of the Cid poem by Frere, and two analyses and versions of the Cid ballads and the Epic : the former by George Dennis, the latter by John Ormsby. Without going so far as Southey, who called the Cid the "finest poem in the Spanish language," or so far as Prescott, who called it "the most remarkable perform-

And so of Lancelot it is said : " Thou were head of all Christian knights ; and thou were the courtiest knight that ever bare shield ; and thou were the truest friend to thy lover that ever bestrode horse ; and thou were the truest lover of

---

ance of the Middle Ages," we must allow that it stands in the very first rank of national poems. Its peculiar value to us is in the fact that it is the earliest of all the great national poems of modern Europe which have reached us in a perfectly unadulterated form, unless we include Beowulf in this number. And if we take the ideal Cid of the romances, chronicle, and poem together, and as he lives in the imagination of the Spanish people, the Cid legend stands at the head of the legendary poetry of Europe. But they who desire to master the poem itself should read the book which Damas Hinard wrote for the Empress Eugénie (Paris, 4to, 1858), the text with a prose version, commentary, and glossary.

a sinful man that ever loved woman ;
and thou were the kindest man that ever
strake with sword ; and thou were the
goodliest person ever came among press
of knights ; and thou were the meekest
man and the gentlest that ever ate in
hall among ladies ; and thou were the
sternest knight to thy mortal foe that
ever put spear in the rest." [1]

Methinks that the tale of the death of
Arthur, Guinevere, and of Lancelot, as
told by Malory, along with the death and
last death-march of the Cid, as told in
the Chronicle, may stand beside the
funeral of Hector, which closes the
Iliad—

ὡς οἵ γ' ἀμφίεπον τάφον Ἕκτορος
ἱπποδάμοιο.[2]

---

[1] σῇ τ' ἀγανοφροσύνῃ, καὶ σοῖς
ἀγανοῖς ἐπέεσσι.—Il. xxiv. 772.

[2] In nothing has the revival of sound
critical taste done better service than in re-

That immense and varied mass of
legend had its religious as well as its
secular side. The Lives of the Saints, of
which the Golden Legend is the cream,
contains, in the theological domain, the
same interminable series of romances,
usually wearisome, always inventive,
and at times nobly poetic, which the
mediæval romances give us in the domain of chivalry. Far more useful his-

calling us to the Arthurian Cycle, the day-
spring of our glorious literature. The clos-
ing books of Malory's Arthur certainly
rank, both in conception and in form, with
the best poetry of Europe ; in quiet pathos
and reserved strength they hold their own
with the epics of any age. Beside this
simple, manly type of the mediæval hero
the figures in the Idylls of the King look
like the dainty Perseus of Canova placed
beside the heroic Theseus of Pheidias.

It is true, as Mr. Matthew Arnold has

4630

torically, and far more closely bound up
with the imaginative literature of Europe,
are the delightful collections of Fabliaux,
the parent of so much in Boccaccio,
Chaucer, even in Rabelais, Shakespeare,
and Molière.   That wonderful storehouse
of the lay and bourgeois spirit of the
thirteenth and fourteenth centuries preserves for us an inimitable picture of

---

said, that poetry and prose are perfectly dis-
tinct forms of utterance.   But the line
which marks off poetry from prose is not
an absolutely rigid one, and we may have
the essentials of poetry without metre or
scansion.   In Malory's Death of Arthur and
Lancelot, or in Chapters of Job and Isaiah
in the English Bible, we have the conceptions, the melody, the winged words, and
inimitable turns of phrase which consti-
tute the highest poetry.   We need a term
to include the best imaginative work in the
most artistic form, and the only English
word left is—poetry.

the knighthood, ladyhood, and yeomanry
of the Middle Ages.[1]

In the real national lays of the old
world, in legend, romance, and tale, in
their first native form, we have a complete history of civilisation : the source
from which Virgil and Livy, Boccaccio
and Chaucer, Shakespeare and Calderon,

---

[1] We have now in 6 vols. the new collection of Fabliaux, by MM. de Montaiglon
and G. Raynaud (Paris, 1872–1886). But
as this, the first complete collection, is
printed from the old MSS. verbatim, it is
of little use except to students of French
literature. The prose version of Legrand
d'Aussy is eminently readable ; but as the
augmented edition of this, by Renouard,
is not now very easily found, an accessible
and popular prose version of these inimitable tales is amongst the pressing wants of
the general reader. And herein the more
outrageous license peculiar to this form of
poetry, might very well disappear.

drew their inspiration, the source of almost all that is most living and true in subsequent art. It is a cycle at once of poetry, of reflection, of manners, the nature of the race flinging itself forth into expression in its own artless way before the canons of poetry were invented, or the race of critics spawned. He to whom this poetry as a whole is familiar, who had heard its full heart throbbing against its sturdy side, would know the great spirits of the human race, and would live in some of its noblest thoughts. And withal, it is so easy, so plain, and fascinating in itself, lying in a few familiar volumes, one-tenth of the bulk of that mountain of literary husks, wherewith men fill themselves as Mudie's cart comes round, chewing rather than reading, careless of method, self-re-straint, or moral aim.

CHAPTER III.

POETS OF THE MODERN WORLD.

MODERN poetry in its developed form opens with the great epic of Catholicism, the *Divina Commedia* of Dante. We Northern people are too ready to treat our own Shakespeare as the poetic embodiment of all that can interest humanity. But what Shakespeare is to the Teutonic races, Dante is to the Latin races. And on certain sides he is far more distinctly the philosopher, the historian, the prophet. He is all this, often in a way which seriously mars his perfection as a poet. But to a student of literature, it is all the more interesting that he so often recalls to us in whole cantos of his poem, now Plato, now Tacitus, now Augustine. The Di-

vine Comedy is no easy task; neither its
language, nor its meaning, nor its design
are always obvious. To most readers it
presents itself as a mystical vision; some
find in it historical satire, others a religious allegory. It reminds us at times
of the Vision of Piers Ploughman, again
of the Pilgrim's Progress, now of the
Apocalypse and the Book of Job, or
again of the *Faery Queen* and *Faust*.
It is all of these and much more. It is
the review in one vast picture of human
life as a whole, and human civilisation
as a whole; all that it had been, was,
and might become, as presented to the
greatest brain and profoundest nature
of the Middle Ages. It is man and the
world seen, it is true, through the Catholic Camera Obscura—a picture intense,
vivid, complete, albeit in a light not
seldom narrow and artificial. Every part
and episode has its double and treble
meaning. And when we have pene-

trated within to know some one or two
of its senses, it is to find that there are
many more wrapped up within its folds
and hidden to our eye. It is a Bible or
Gospel—Bible and Gospel without reve-
lation or canonical authority, and, like
the older Bible, full of mystery and difficulty; but, none the less, in spite of
mysteriousness and difficulties, especially
fitted for the daily study of all who can
read with patience, insight, and single-
ness of heart. As it has been said of
other books that move us deeply, "in
quietness and confidence shall be your
strength."

There is an entire library of Dantesque
literature, mostly to my mind needless.
But it must be remembered that few
readers can enjoy Dante perfectly without the assistance of some translation or
notes of some kind. Mr. Ruskin once
hazarded the glorious paradox that
Cary's Dante was better reading than

Milton's *Paradise Lost.* Cary is useful
for Dante, just as Conington is useful
for Virgil; but it can hardly be called
poetry. The other verse translations of
Dante I can only read as "cribs." Dr.
John Carlyle's admirable prose version
of the *Inferno* has been completed by
the *Purgatorio* and the *Paradiso* of
A. J. Butler, making an almost perfect
English version. For my own part I
prefer Lamennais' translation of the Divine Comedy into antique French prose,
the effect of which is at once weird and
solemn. This, with the brief notes in
the Florentine edition, and what the two
Carlyles and Dean Church have written,
and the diligent reading of Dante himself, including his *Vita Nuova* (Rossetti's
excellent translation), and the rest of his
prose, should be better than the entire
Dantesque library which has grown up
round the poem. The most melancholy
of all superstitions is that which restricts

the reading of Dante to the *Inferno*, and even to a few famous episodes in that. The *Inferno* alone gives no adequate idea of Dante's social conceptions. The *Purgatorio* is, to my mind, the most profound, as well as the most beautiful part of all the work of Dante.

The first commentator on Dante, Boccaccio, has left us the earliest perfect example of modern prose ; on one side of it, still the most beautiful of modern prose, that which in music and native grace comes nearest to the prose of Plato. The immortal stories of the *Decameron* have that rich glow of the wit and grace of the Middle Ages, that aroma of full-blossoming life which binds us with its spell in the Italian dramas of Shakespeare, and which is so near akin to the Italian mastery of the arts of form. The *Decameron*, as belongs to its age and the whole Fabliaux literature from which it sprung, is redolent of that

libertine humanism which stamps the
Renascence; but not a few of its tales are
free from offence, and there are published selections which may fitly be read
by the young.[1]

The great Italian epics of Ariosto and
Tasso, and the lyrics of Petrarch, have
exercised over the ages which they have
charmed, and over the races whom they
have inspired, an influence as profound
and humanising as any which poetry has
ever exerted. We, whose imagination
has been trained by darker and fiercer
types, do not easily fall in with the
poetic sources of the Southern passion
for sentiment and colour. But though

---

[1] Amongst others there is a small selection for the use of schools (Turin, 1882,
8vo). Boccaccio's language and meaning
are so easy that neither translation nor
commentary is needed, nor do I know of
any worth reading.

this Italian poetry is in a world far other from ours of to-day, and though much of it is in a form artificial to our taste, its importance in literature and in history should give it a place in any systematic course of reading.[1]

---

[1] No one in this century seems to read the English translations of the Italian epics in rhymed heroics in imitation of Mr. Pope and Mr. Dryden, which were so much in vogue in the last century, or those which in imitation of Chapman were in vogue in the century preceding. It must be allowed that they are rather meritorious performances than good reading; but it was better to read Ariosto and Tasso so than not to read them at all. I feel the same even of the many really excellent versions of Petrarch's sonnets. But the subtle complexity and charm of the Petrarchian sonnet is as incommunicable as that of Horace. Yet one would like to see a version by Mr. Swinburne.

In the later Italian poets there are no unfrequent bursts of true poetry, as if from time to time the great lyre of old ages gave forth of itself some strange spontaneous air, where it hung fixed as a trophy of the past, though there be none who dare take it from its resting-place, or strike the chords of the departed masters.[1]

As for French poetry, apart from the glorious lyrics of the older language, some exquisite echoes of which have been heard again in our own age, the world-wide and world-abiding masterpieces are to be found in the long roll of the dramatists of France. The French drama is,

---

[1] And that in spite of the beautiful things of Filicaja, Leopardi, and Manzoni, whose *Cinque Maggio* surpasses that of Byron almost as much as his *Promessi Sposi* falls short of the *Bride of Lammermoor.*

to the ordinary English reader, one of
the stumbling-blocks of literature. He
finds it universally counted amongst the
classics of modern Europe, and most
justly so; he gathers that it exerts a profound fascination and influence over the
French race; he can perceive its symmetry and subtle art of style. But he
does not enjoy it, and he does not read it,
and, except when some famous "star"
is performing, he does not care to hear
it from the stage. And whether he
listens to it, or reads it, he inevitably
ends with that most futile resource,
some trite and *banal* comparison with
Shakespeare. Glorious Will has not a
little to answer for, in that, most unwit-
tingly, he has stopped up the ears of his
countrymen to some of the most perfect
moods of the lyre, which chanced to be
those he never struck. There is much
in the method and genius of the French
drama which falls chill and stark on

ears accustomed to the abounding life of
a Shakespearean play. He who begins
by comparing the two methods is lost;
he might as well compare an Italian
garden and a tropical forest. To enjoy
these French dramas in all their subtle
finish requires perhaps for an English-
man a more special study of their
peculiar poetic form than most readers
can give. The French drama, like the
Greek and the Roman, is to the typical
drama of Spain, England, and Germany
what a statue is to a picture. Neither
lyrical wealth of imagery, nor rapidity
of action, nor multiplicity and contrast
of situations, nor subtle involution of
motive, are the instruments of art em-
ployed. The dominant aim is to produce one massive impression; the artistic
instrument is harmony of tone; the form
is consistently ideal, never realistic. The
realism and movement which we look
for in a play are as alien to the classical

drama as trousers and boots to a classical statue.

Even if the French classical plays had less poetic power of their own, they would still hold a high place in any serious scheme of reading for their historical and ethical value. They form the most systematic and successful effort ever made in literature to idealise in modern poetry the great types of character and race, as they move in one unending procession across the general history of mankind. They epitomise civilisation in a regular series of striking tableaux of the past, and of the East ; so that they hold up the mirror (not quite successfully to Nature), but to the successive phases of human society and the moral power and tone of each. Thus judged, in spite of some serious defects and much coldness, yet by the innate grandeur of his soul, the statuesque unity of form, and by virtue of the profound moral impression which he has left on his countrymen, Corneille remains one of the greatest of modern poets.

The even superior grace, tenderness, and versatility of Racine make him a more popular favourite. It is not necessary to enter on the secular debate to which of the rivals the palm is to be given. Voltaire, with all his inferiority to both, carried out in a form which suits the genius of his language and people the design of the elder dramatists, to idealise for our modern world most remote and different types of human life. Dryden and Otway in England attempted the same purpose ; Metastasio and Alfieri were more successful in Italy ; Goethe and Schiller revived it in Germany. It cannot be pronounced a true success in the hands of any of them. Doubtless, it remains for the future to show us all that awaits human genius in this magnificent field of art—the idealisation of the past in a form at once poetic and true. Scott may be said to have accomplished it in prose for considerable epochs and phases of the past. No one can pretend that even Shakespeare did anything in this sphere at all worthy of himself; or indeed that he had any adequate sense of the problem. With all their shortcomings and their tolerance of academic conventions, the French dramatists afford us the most serious, and on the whole the most successful, example of a real historical poetry.

The same earnestness of purpose and systematic method distinguish also the old comic drama of France. Justice has been done to the inimitable genius of Molière. It may be doubted if justice has yet been done to his power as philosopher, moralist, and teacher. As profound a master of human nature on its brighter side as Shakespeare himself, he gives us an even more complete and sys-

tematic analysis of modern society, and
a still larger gallery of its familiar types.
Inexhaustible good nature, imperturbable
good sense, instinctive aversion to folly,
affectation, meanness, and untruth, ever
mark Molière ; he is always humane,
courteous, sound of heart ; he is never
savage, morose, cynical, or obscene ; he
has neither the mad ribaldry of Aristophanes, nor the mad rage of Swift ; he
never ceases to be a man, wise, tender,
and good in every fibre, even whilst we
feel the darker mood of pensive perplex-
ity that human frivolity perpetually
awakens in his soul.

Men will continue to ask if his great
masterpiece, the *Misanthrope*, be pure
comedy or serious drama ; if the poet
intended to justify *Alceste*, or to excuse
Philinte. Doubtless both fountains of
feeling well up in him, as he meditates
on the insoluble problems of artificial
society and the eternal dilemmas of

social compromise. The systematic and philosophic spirit of Molière strike us emphatically if we take the whole collection of his plays, and see how distinctly each type of character is in turn presented to our eyes, and how complete and various the entire series appears. No other painter of manners has given us a gallery of portraits so carefully classed. But the measure of Molière is hardly to be taken till we see him presented at the Comédie Française ; where a long tradition of actors and critics, combining with each other, produces the most perfect embodiment of the scenic art which the modern stage has achieved.

The prolific drama of Spain is certainly, from a national and ethical point of view, more interesting than the classical drama of France. In variety, imaginative energy, and *brio*, it is surpassed only by our own. It has exerted an even more manifold and permanent hold over the minds of its own people. And in its association with the religion of the people, their profoundest religious belief, as well as their inmost religious feeling, the Spanish drama has a quality which gives that supreme dignity to the drama of Athens, but which, since the Middle Ages, has been lost elsewhere to the drama of Europe. The Spanish drama by its wonderful originality and variety is certainly one of the most striking phenomena in the history of poetry. It is melancholy to think how complete is the neglect of a literature so rich and rare. Of late Calderon is beginning to be better known. His magnificent imagination, his infinite fertility, his power and passion have a real Shakespearean note ; whilst his purity and devotional fervour remind us of the Catholic period of Corneille's career. In our own day he has exercised the skill of a crowd of translators. Shelley gave us a fine fragment from the *Magician;* Trench, M'Carthy, and others have tried their hands on one of the most difficult problems in the art of translation. But the English reader can obtain some adequate conception of Calderon from the eight plays of which an admirably poetic version has been given us by Edward Fitzgerald, the translator, or paraphrast, of Omar Kayyam. If Fitzgerald's accuracy had equalled his ingenuity, he might claim the very first place amongst modern translators.[1] Auguste Comte had so high

---

[1] It is much to be regretted that except the *Mayor of Zalamea,* the *Wonder-working Magician,* and *Life is a Dream,* the two latter in the second series, Fitzgerald deliberately selected the less important dramas. The seven selected by Comte as types out of the nearly two hundred surviving pieces are : La Vida es sueño, El Alcalde de Zalamea, A secreto agravio

an opinion of the Spanish dramatists that, in the midst of his philosophic labours, he made a selection of twenty plays from different poets, a work edited by his friend, J. S. Florez, and published in Paris in 1854 (Teatro Español).

One production of the Spanish imagination alone has obtained universal rank amongst the great masterpieces of the world. Cervantes carried to the highest point that pensive and prophetic spirit which seems to mark all the greater humourists, unless it be Aristophanes in his wilder moods. Like Rabelais and Molière, like Shakespeare and Fielding, Cervantes is ever reminding us, in the loudest peals of our mirth, that life is

---

secreta venganza, No siempre lo peor es cierto, Mañanas de abril y mayo, La Nave del Mercader, La Viña del Señor. Of these, the first and second have been translated by Fitzgerald.

full of mystery and of struggle. But none of these profound spirits have handled the problems of life with greater breadth or more noble tenderness than the author of *Don Quixote*. This inimitable work is the serio-comic analogue of Dante's Vision. It is a burlesque divine comedy: the survey of human society, its types of character, and its moral problems, at a moment when one great phase of history was giving way to another. Of this glorious work we now have a really adequate version in the admirable translation by Mr. J. Ormsby. The true Don Quixote presents to us the secular contest between the past and the present. This great creation is as much history and philosophy as it is romance or comedy. It idealises the doubt and wonder bred in the soul of its heroic author, a soldier at once of the old world and of the new, one who united the crusading instinct of the Cid with the practical genius of Molière; who saw clearly the inevitable conflict between the old world of chivalry and the new world of industry and science; and sympathising with both, felt a clear and conscious mission to announce to chivalry its inexorable doom, teaching the new world withal what it lacked of chivalry and heroism. And, uniting in himself at once good sense and chivalry, Cervantes points out to us at last a possible union of these two.

The poets of Germany need not detain us. Germany has indeed but one great poet of European rank, the encyclopædic Goethe, whose exquisite lyrics and the inexhaustible *Faust* are a constant refreshment to the thoughtful spirit. The wonderful intellectual impulse which Goethe gave to all forms of literature in his generation, doubtless the most important of the whole nineteenth century, has caused rather an excessive than a deficient estimate of his direct work as a poet. The other German poets are often graceful and learned ; we read them conscientiously when we first acquire the language, and their delightful ballads continually exercise the ingenuity of translators, both domestic and public. But except to the lovely lyrics of Goethe and Heine, I venture to doubt if many of us return to them with increasing zest. In the present day they get possibly an even excessive attention from those who, like many young persons, have never read a line of Dante, Ariosto, Chaucer, or Calderon.

Of our English poets there is little that needs to be said, all the more that a dominant school of criticism now guides the public taste in this matter with consummate judgment ; and that the general interest in poetry is perhaps at once wider and more healthy than it has ever been at any period of our history. The best estimates of our great masterpieces have been reduced to a popular form in the admirable hand book of Mr. S. A. Brooke, and the judgment of Mr. Matthew Arnold in poetry is almost as much a final verdict as that of Sainte-Beuve himself.   Here and there specialists and partisans worry us with exaggeration and hobbies of their own.   But, as a rule, the position of the greater poets is perfectly established and clearly understood.   It is no pretension of these few pages to do more than utter a few words of plea for reading at any rate the best.

Even of Shakespeare himself it is better to recognise frankly the truth, that he is by no means always at his best, and occasionly produces quite unworthy stuff.   No poet known to us was so careless of his genius, so little jealous of his own work, and none has left his creations in a form so unauthentic and confused ; for no one of his plays was published with his name in his lifetime. Let us face the necessity, that it is better in such case to know his eight or ten masterpieces thoroughly, rather than to treat his thirty-six supposed pieces with equal irreverent veneration. With Milton the case is different. In the *Paradise Lost* and in the *Lyrics*—lyrics unsurpassed in all poetry, and for Englishmen, at least, the high-water mark of lyrical perfection, equally faultless in their poetic form and in their moral charm, the poet seems to be putting his whole inspiration into every line and almost every phrase. And thus, till his strength began to wane with life, this most self-possessed of the poets hardly ever swerves or swoops in his calm majestic flight.

Of our poets, and especially of our modern poets, there is happily now but little need to speak. All serious readers are sufficiently agreed. That Burns,

Byron, Shelley, Keats, and Wordsworth belong, each in his way and each in his degree, to the perpetual glories of our literature, is no longer open to doubt. No one needs any pressing to read Coleridge, Scott, Tennyson, and Browning ; they have all enjoyed an ample, almost an excessive, recognition in their own lifetime. But a little word may be spoken in season respecting our honored Laureate—a word which the critics keep too much to themselves. There is danger lest conventional adulation and a certain unique quality of his may tend to mislead the general public as to the true place of Tennyson amongst poets. Since the death of Wordsworth he has stood, beyond all question, in a class wholly by himself, far above all contemporary lyric poets. It is no less certain that he, alone of the Victorians, has definitely entered the immortal group of our English poets, and stands beside Wordsworth, Coleridge, and Keats. Nay, we must go further than this. Tennyson has a gift of melody in meditative lyric, more subtle and exquisite than any poet but Shakespeare and Shelley. He has, moreover, a *curiosa felicitas* of phrase, a finished grace, sustained over the whole of *In Memoriam*, which is peculiarly rare in English poetry ; one which reminds us of the unerring certainty of touch in Horace, Racine, Heine, and Leopardi. But this delightful quality is a somewhat late product of any literature, and is seldom found with equal power of imagination. The Laureate has had the good fortune to live in an epoch of amazing fecundity, and to embody in graceful verse the originality and fervour of an original and fervid age. The young, brimful of the hopes and feelings which teem in our time, are eager to hail a poet who is in many ways to the cultivated class of our time that which Victor Hugo has been to the French people. They are apt to forget that a unique gift of melody and an undertone of sentimental philosophising does not amount to imaginative power of the very first rank. When we survey calmly the more ambitious pieces of this exquisite lyrist, such as that somewhat boudoir epic, the *Idylls of the King;* the conventional dramas, and the facile ballads of his decline, we find ourselves in the presence of a mind where the power of expression outweighs the thought : one that can strike out little of a really high type, either in character, in narration, or in drama. These consummately graceful verses have none of that wealth of imagination, that flashing insight into life, that tragic thunderpeal, which often, it may be, with far less chastened diction, are revealed to us by the mighty spirits of Scott, Byron, and Goethe. Let us read our Tennyson and be thankful, without supposing, like some young ladies' pet curate, that this is the high-water mark of English poetry.

Finally, as to prose romances, the same principles will serve, though they are even more difficult to apply. Read the best. Our great eighteenth century novelists have won a place in the abiding literature of the world—a place beside the poets more specially so called. Their knowledge of human nature, their humour, their dramatic skill, their pathos, make them peers of those who have used the forms of verse, and it is in the form and not in substance that they may rank below the masters of the creative art in verse. First among them all is the generous soul of Fielding, to whom so much is forgiven for the nobleness of his great heart. On him and on the others there rests the curse of their age, and no incantation can reverse the sen-

tence pronounced upon those who deliberately stoop to the unclean. It is a
grave defect in the splendid tale of *Tom
Jones*—of all prose romances the most
rich in life and the most artistic in con-
struction—that a Bowdlerised version of
it would be hardly intelligible as a tale.
Grossness, alas ! has entered into the
marrow of its bones. Happily, vice has
not ; and amidst much that is repulsive,
we feel the good man's reverence for
goodness, and the humane spirit's honour
of every humane quality, whilst the pure
figure of the womanly Sophia (most womanly of all women in fiction) walks in
maiden meditation across the darkest
scenes, as the figure of the glorified
Gretchen passes across the revel in the
Walpurgis-Nacht.

The same century too gave us (and
without any of its defects two immortal masterpieces of creative art—
the exquisite idyll of Goldsmith and

the original conception of Defoe. We
are so familiar with the *Vicar of Wakefield* and *Robinson Crusoe* that we are
too ready to forget their extraordinary
influence over the whole European mind.
We are hardly sensible that both contain
noble lessons for every age. *Robinson
Crusoe*, which is a fairy tale to the child,
a book of adventure to the young, is a
work on social philosophy to the mature.
It is a picture of civilisation. The essential moral attributes of man, his innate impulses as a social being, his absolute dependence on society, even as a
solitary individual, his subjection to the
physical world, and his alliance with the
animal world, the statical elements of
social philosophy, and the germs of
man's historical evolution have never
been touched with more sagacity, and
assuredly have never been idealised with
such magical simplicity and truth. It
remains, with *Don Quixote*, the only

prose work of the fancy which has equal charms for every age of life, and which has inexhaustible teaching for the student of man and of society.

Of Walter Scott one need as little speak as of Shakespeare. He belongs to mankind, to every age and race, and he certainly must be counted as in the first line of the great creative minds of the world. His unique glory is to have definitely succeeded in the ideal reproduction of historical types, so as to preserve at once beauty, life, and truth, a task which neither Ariosto and Tasso, nor Corneille and Racine, nor Alfieri, nor Goethe and Schiller—no! nor even Shakespeare himself entirely achieved. It is true that their instrument was the more exacting one of verse, whilst Scott's was prose. But in brilliancy of conception, in wealth of character, in dramatic art, in glow and harmony of colour, Scott put forth all the powers of a mas-

ter poet. His too early death, like that
of Shakespeare, leaves on us a cruel
sense of the inexhaustible quality of his
imagination. Prodigious excess in work
destroyed in full maturity that splendid
brain, and to the last he had magnificent bursts of his old power. But for
this the imagination of Scott might have
continued to range over the boundless
field of human history. What we have
is mainly of the Middle Ages, the genius
of chivalry in all its colour and moral
beauty ; but he had no exclusive spirit
and no crude doctrines. And as Cervantes is ever reminding us how much
of the mediæval chivalry was doomed,
so Scott, whilst singing the same plain-
tive death-chant, is for ever reminding
us how much of it is destined to endure.

The genius of Scott has raised up a
school of historical romance ; and though
the best work of Chateaubriand, Manzoni, and Bulwer may take rank as true

art, the endless crowd of inferior imitations are nothing but a weariness to the flesh. A far higher place in the permanent field of beauty belongs to the work of Miss Edgeworth, Miss Austen, and George Eliot, who have founded a new school of romantic art, with the subtle observation, the delicate shades of character, and the indescribable *finesse* peculiarly adapted to women's work. These admirable pictures of society hold a rare and abiding place in English literature.

But assuredly black night will quickly cover the vast bulk of modern fiction—work as perishable as the generations whose idleness it has amused. It belongs not to the great creations of the world. Beside them it is flat and poor. Such facts in human nature as it reveals are trivial and special in themselves, and for the most part abnormal and unwholesome. I stand beside the ceaseless flow of this miscellaneous torrent as one

stands watching the turbid rush of
Thames at London Bridge, wondering
whence it all comes, whither it all goes,
what can be done with it, and what
may be its ultimate function in the order
of providence. To a reader who would
nourish his taste on the boundless har-
vests of the poetry of mankind, this
sewage outfall of to-day offers as little in
creative as in moral value. Lurid and
irregular streaks of imagination, extravagance of plot and incident, petty and
mean subjects of study, forced and un-
natural situations, morbid pathology of
crime, dull copying of the dullest commonplace, melodramatic hurly - burly,
form the certain evidence of an art that
is exhausted, produced by men and
women to whom it is become a mere
trade, in an age wherein change and ex-
citement have corrupted the power of
pure enjoyment.

Genius, industry, subtlety, and in-

genuity have (it must yet be acknowl-
edged) thrown their best into the fiction
of to-day ; and not a few works of undeniable brilliancy and vigour have been
produced. Of course everybody reads,
and every one enjoys, Dickens, Thackeray, Bulwer, the Brontës, Trollope,
George Eliot. Far be it from any man,
even the severest student, to eschew
them. There are no doubt typical works
of theirs which will ultimately be recognised as within the immortal cycle of
English literature, in the nobler sense of
this term. He would be a bold man
who should say that *Pickwick* and *Vanity Fair*, the *Last Days of Pompeii* and
Jane Eyre, the *Last Chronicle of Barset*
and *Silas Marner*, will never take rank
in the roll which opens with *Tom Jones*
and *Clarissa*, the *Vicar* and *Tristram
Shandy*. It may be that the future will
find in them insight into nature and
beauty of creative form, such as belongs

to the order of all high imaginative art. But as yet we are too near and too little dispassionate to decide this matter to-day. And, in the meantime, the indiscriminate zest for these delightful writers of our age too often dulls our taste for the undoubted masters of the world.

Certain it is that much, very much, of these fascinating moderns has neither the stamp of abiding beauty, nor the saving grace of moral truth. Dickens, alas! soon passed into a mannerism of artificial whimsicalities, alternating with shallow melodrama. Thackeray wearies his best lovers by a cynical monotony of meanness. By grace of a very rare genius, the best work of the Brontës is saved, as by fire, out of the repulsive sensationalism they started, destined to perish in shilling dreadfuls. Trollope only now and then rises, as by a miracle, out of his craft as an industrious recorder of pleasant commonplace. And even George Eliot, conscientious artist as she is, too often wrote as if she were sinking under the effort to live up to her early reputation. On all of these the special evils of their time weigh more or less. They write too often as if it were their publishers and not their genius which prompted the work ; or as if their task were to provide a new set of puzzles in rare psychological problems.

In romance every one can write something ; clever men and women can write smart things, extremely clever men and women can write remarkable things. And thus, whilst so large a part of the educated world writes fiction, what we get even from the best is too often sensational, morbid, sardonic, artificial, trivial, or mean. We all read them and shall continue to read them ; and thousands of tales which have far inferior quality. But they lack the moral and social insight of true romance. They are not the stuff of which our daily reading should consist. They are destined for the most part to a not very distant oblivion. When a regular training of the poetic capacity shall have become general, their enormous vogue will be over. In the meantime let each of us deal with them as he finds right, remembering this, that they can hardly claim a place as an indispensable part of our serious education.

In substance the same thing holds good of the foreign romances of our own generation. Neither German, Italian, nor Spanish fiction, so far as I know, can pretend to a place beside the modern fiction of England and France. And he would be a bold patriot who should rank the fiction of England, since the death of Scott, above that of Victor Hugo, George Sand, Balzac, Mérimée, Théophile Gautier, and Dumas. But the wonderful powers of all these are unhappily counterbalanced by the defects of their qualitics. If Victor Hugo be in the sum the greatest European literary force since Goethe and Scott, the readers of his prose have too often to suffer from rank stage balderdash. Balzac wearies us all by a sardonic monotony of wickedness; George Sand by an unwomanly proneness to idealise lust. *Notre Dame* and *Les Misérables*, *Père Goriot* and *Eugénie Grandet*, *Consuelo* and *La Mare aux Diables*, *Capitaine Fracasse* and *Vingt Ans Après* are books of extraordinary vigour ; but it would seem to me treason against art to rank even the best of them with immortal masterpieces, such as *Tom Jones* and the *Vicar of Wakefield.*

Contemporary English romance, however insipid and crude in art, is usually wholesome, or at worst harmless ; but what words remain for the typical French novel which at present fills the place of reading to so large a part of educated Europe ? By the accident of language the French novel is written, not for Frenchmen, but for all men of culture and leisure ; its world is not the real world of Frenchmen at all, but an artificial world of cosmopolitan origin, which has its conventional home on the boulevards ; its writers are not the leaders of French literature, but a special school of feuilletonists. It is intensely smart, diabolically ingenious, and with a really masterly command of its own peculiar style and method. Beside it the raw stuff which dribbles incessantly into the circulating libraries of England, Germany, and America, is the work of amateurs who are still learning the difficulties of their own trade. But with all this skill, it is to me even more unreadable. The contortions it makes in its efforts to twist out novel situations; the mere literary knowingness, the monotonous variations on its one string of adultery—adultery without love, senti-

ment, or excuse ; a purely conventional
and feuilleton kind of adultery, existing
nowhere in nature, unless it be in some
gambling centre of blackguardly "high
life ;" its want of any trace of what can
be justly regarded as real art, or as real
human nature — all these make the
"French novel" to me more unapproach-
able than a Leipsic edition of the Apos-
tolic Fathers.   Men of brains and knowledge read it—read it, we know, daily ;
just as they smoke cavendish, and as the
French subaltern takes absinthe.   But
no one enjoys it.   *Non ragioniam di lor,
non guarda, ma passa.*   To be addicted
to it, is a vice ; to manufacture it, is a
crime.   They are not books, these things.
To imbibe this compound, is not to read.

In Europe, as in England, Walter
Scott remains as yet the last in the series
of the great creative spirits of the human
race.   No one of his successors, however
clear be the genius and the partial suc-

cess of some of them, belongs to the same grand type of mind, or has now a lasting place in the roll of the immortals. It should make us sad to reflect that a generation, which already has begun to treat Scott with the indifference that is the lot of a " a classic," should be ready to fill its insatiable maw with the ephemeral wares of the booksellers, and the reeking garbage of the boulevard.

We all read Scott's romances, as we have all read Hume's History of England; but how often do we read them, how zealously, with what sympathy and understanding? I am told that the last discovery of modern culture is that Scott's prose is commonplace; that the young men at our universities are far too critical to care for his artless sentences and flowing descriptions. They prefer Mr. Swinburne, Mr. Mallock, and the Euphuism of young Oxford, just as some people prefer a Dresden Shepherdess to the Caryatides of the Erechtheum, pronounce Fielding to be low, and Mozart to be *passé*. As boys love lollypops, so these juvenile fops love to roll phrases about under the tongue, as if phrases in themselves had a value apart from thoughts, feelings, great conceptions, or human sympathy. For Scott is just one of the poets (we may call poets all the great creators in prose or in verse) of whom one never wearies, just as one can listen to Beethoven, or watch the sunrise or the sunset day by day with new delight. I think I can read the *Antiquary* or the *Bride of Lammermoor*, *Ivanhoe*, *Quentin Durward*, and *Old Mortality* at least once a year afresh.

Scott is a perfect library in himself. A constant reader of romances would find that it needed months to go through even the best pieces of the inexhaustible painter of eight full centuries and every type of man; and he might repeat the

process of reading him ten times in a
lifetime without a sense of fatigue or
sameness. The poetic beauty of Scott's
creations is almost the least of his great
qualities. It is the universality of his
sympathy that is so truly great, the justice of his estimates, the insight into the
spirit of each age, his intense absorption
of self in the vast epic of human civilisation. What are the old almanacs that
they so often give us as histories beside
these living pictures of the ordered succession of ages? As in Homer himself,
we see in this prose Iliad of modern history, the battle of the old and the new,
the heroic defence of ancient strongholds,
the long impending and inevitable doom
of mediæval life. Strong men and proud
women struggle against the destiny of
modern society, unconsciously working
out its ways, undauntedly defying its
power. How just is our island Homer!
Neither Greek nor Trojan sways him;

Achilles is his hero; Hector is his fa-
vorite ; he loves the counsels of chiefs,
and the palace of Priam; but the swine-
herd, the charioteer, the slave girl, the
hound, the beggar, and the herdsman,
all glow alike in the harmonious coloring
of his peopled epic. We see the dawn of
our English nation, the defence of Christ-
endom against the Koran, the grace
and the terror of feudalism, the rise of
monarchy out of baronies, the rise
of parliaments out of monarchy, the
rise of industry out of serfage, the
pathetic ruin of chivalry, the splendid
death-struggle of Catholicism, the sylvan
tribes of the mountain (remnants of our
pre-historic forefathers) beating themselves to pieces against the hard advance
of modern industry; we see the grim heroism of the Bible-martyrs, the catastrophe
of feudalism overwhelmed by a practical age which knew little of its graces
and almost nothing of its virtues. Such

is Scott, who, we may say, has done for
the various phases of modern history,
what Shakespeare has done for the
manifold types of human character.
And this glorious and most human and
most historical of poets, without whom
our very conception of human develop-
ment would have ever been imperfect,
this manliest, and truest, and widest, of
romances we neglect for some hothouse
hybrid of psychological analysis, for the
wretched imitators of Balzac, and the
jackanapes phrasemongering of some
Osric of the day, who assures us that
Scott is an absolute Philistine.

CHAPTER IV.

THE MISUSE OF BOOKS.

In speaking with enthusiasm of Scott, as of Homer, or of Shakespeare, or of Milton, or of any of the accepted masters of the world, I have no wish to insist dogmatically upon any single name, or two or three in particular. Our enjoyment and reverence of the great poets of the world is seriously injured nowadays by the habit we get of singling out some particular quality, some particular school of art, for intemperate praise, or, still worse, for intemperate abuse. Mr. Ruskin, I suppose, is answerable for the taste for this one-sided and spasmodic criticism; he asks readers to cast aside Coleridge, Shelley, and Byron, and to stick to—such goody-goody verses as

Evangeline and the *Angel in the House.*
And now every young gentleman who
has the trick of a few adjectives will
languidly vow that Marlowe is supreme,
or Murillo foul. It is the mark of rational criticism, as well as of healthy
thought, to maintain an evenness of
mind in judging of great works, to recognise great qualities in due proportion, to
feel that defects are made up by beauties, and beauties are often balanced by
weakness. The true judgment implies a
weighing of each work and each work-
man as a whole, in relation to the sum
of human cultivation and the gradual
advance of the movement of ages. And
in this matter we shall usually find that
the world is right, the world of the
modern centuries and the nations of
Europe together. It is unlikely, to say
the least of it, that a young person who
has hardly ceased making Latin verses
will be able to reverse the decisions of

the civilised world; and it is even more
unlikely that Milton and Molière, Fielding and Scott, will ever be displaced by
a poet who has unaccountably lain hid
for one or two centuries. I know, that
in the style of to-day, I ought hardly to
venture to speak about poetry unless I
am prepared to unfold the mysterious
beauties of some unknown genius who
has recently been unearthed by the
Children of Light and Sweetness. I
confess I have no such discovery to announce. I prefer to dwell in Gath and
to pitch my tents in Ashdod; and I
doubt the use of the sling as a weapon
in modern war. I decline to go into
hyperbolic eccentricities over unknown
geniuses, and a single quality or power
is not enough to rouse my enthusiasm.
It is possible that no master ever painted
a buttercup like this one, or the fringe
of a robe like that one; that this poet
has a unique subtlety, and that an unde-

finable music. I am still unconvinced,
though the man who cannot see it, we
are told, should at once retire to the
place where there is wailing and gnashing of teeth.

I am against all gnashing of teeth,
whether for or against a particular idol.
I stand by the men, and by all the men,
who have moved mankind to the depths
of their souls, who have taught generations, and formed our life. If I say of
Scott, that to have drunk in the whole of
his glorious spirit is a liberal education
in itself, I am asking for no exclusive de-
votion to Scott, to any poet, or any school
of poets, or any age, or any country, to
any style or any order of poet, one more
than another. They are as various, for-
tunately, and as many-sided as human
nature itself. If I delight in Scott, I
love Fielding, and Richardson, and
Sterne, and Goldsmith, and Defoe.
Yes, and I will add Cooper and Marryat,

Miss Edgeworth and Miss Austen—to confine myself to those who are already classics, to our own language, and to one form of art alone, and not to venture on the ground of contemporary romance in general. What I have said of Homer, I would say in a degree, but somewhat lower, of those great ancients who are the most accessible to us in English— Æschylus, Aristophanes, Virgil, and Horace. We need not so worship Shakespeare as to neglect Calderon, Molière, Corneille, Racine, Voltaire, Alfieri, Goethe, those dramatists, in many forms, and with genius the most diverse, who have so steadily set themselves to idealise the great types of public life and of the phases of human history. What I have said of Milton I would say of Dante, of Ariosto, of Petrarch, and of Tasso; and in a measure I would say it of Boccaccio and Chaucer, of Camoëns and Spenser, of Rabelais and of Cervantes,

of Gil Blas and the Vicar of Wakefield,
of Byron and of Shelley, of Goethe and
of Schiller.

I protest that I am devoted to no
school in particular : I condemn no
school, I reject none. I am for the
school of all the great men ; and I am
against the school of the smaller men. I
care for Wordsworth as well as for Byron, for Burns as well as Shelley, for
Boccaccio as well as for Milton, for Bun-
yan as well as Rabelais, for Cervantes as
well as for Dante, for Corneille as well
as for Shakespeare, for Goldsmith as
well as Goethe. I stand by the sentence
of the world ; and I hold that in a matter so human and so broad as the highest poetry the judgment of the nations of
Europe is pretty well settled, at any rate
after a century or two of continuous
reading and discussing. Let those who
will assure us that no one can pretend to
culture, unless he swear by Fra Angelico

and Sandro Botticelli, by Arnolpho the son of Lapo, or the Lombardic bricklayers, by Martini and Galuppi (all, by the way, admirable men of the second rank) ; and so, in literature and poetry, there are some who will hear of nothing but Webster or Marlowe ; Blake, Herrick, or Villon ; William Langland or the Earl of Surrey ; Guido Cavalcanti or Omar Kayyam. All of these are men of genius, and each with a special and inimitable gift of his own. But the busy world, which does not hunt poets as collectors hunt for curios, may fairly reserve these lesser lights for the time when they know the greatest well.

So, I say, think mainly of the greatest, of the best known, of those who cover the largest area of human history and man's common nature. Now when we come to count up these poets accepted by the unanimous voice of Europe, we have some thirty or forty names, and amongst

them are some of the most voluminous
of writers. I have been running over
but one department of literature alone—
the poetic. I have been naming those
only, whose names are household words
with us, and the poets for the most part
of modern Europe. Yet even here we
have a list which is usually found in not
less than a hundred volumes at least.
Now poetry and the highest kind of romance are exactly that order of literature
which not only will bear to be read many
times, but that of which the true value
can only be gained by frequent, and indeed habitual, reading. A man can
hardly be said to know the 12th Mass or
the 9th Symphony, by virtue of having
once heard them played ten years ago ;
he can hardly be said to take air and exercise because he took a country walk
once last autumn. And so, he can hardly
be said to know Scott or Shakespeare,
Molière or Cervantes, when he once read

them since the close of his schooldays,
or amidst the daily grind of his professional life. The immortal and universal
poets of our race are to be read and re-
read till their music and their spirit are
a part of our nature; they are to be
thought over and digested till we live in
the world they created for us; they are
to be read devoutly, as devout men read
their Bible and fortify their hearts with
psalms. For as the old Hebrew singer
heard the heavens declare the glory of
their Maker, and the firmament showing
his handiwork, so in the long roll of poetry we see transfigured the strength and
beauty of humanity, the joys and sor-
rows, the dignity and struggles, the long
life-history of our common kind.

I have said but little of the more difficult poetry, and the religious meditations
of the great idealists in prose and verse,
whom it needs a concentrated study to
master. Some of these are hard to all

men, and at all seasons. The Divine
Comedy, in its way, reaches as deep in
its thoughtfulness as Descartes himself.
But these books, if they are difficult to
all, are impossible to the gluttons of the
circulating library. To these munchers
of vapid memoirs and monotonous tales
such books are closed indeed. The
power of enjoyment and of understanding is withered up within them. To the
besotted gambler on the turf the lonely
hillside glowing with heather grows to
be as dreary as a prison ; and so, too, a
man may listen nightly to burlesques,
till *Fidelio* inflicts on him intolerable
fatigue. One may be a devourer of
books, and be actually incapable of reading a hundred lines of the wisest and the
most beautiful. To read one of such
books comes only by habit, as prayer is
impossible to one who habitually dreads
to be alone.

In an age of steam it seems almost

idle to speak of Dante, the most profound, the most meditative, the most
prophetic of all poets, in whose epic the
panorama of mediæval life, of feudalism
at its best, and Christianity at its best,
stands, as in a microcosm, transfigured,
judged, and measured. To most men
the *Paradise Lost*, with all its mighty
music and its idyllic pictures of human
nature, of our first child-parents in their
naked purity and their awakening
thought, is a serious and ungrateful
task—not to be ranked with the simple
enjoyments ; it is a possession to be acquired only by habit. The great religious poets, the imaginative teachers of
the heart, are never easy reading. But
the reading of them is a religious habit,
rather than an intellectual effort. I
pretend not to be dealing with a matter
so deep and high as religion, or indeed
with education in the fuller sense. I
will say nothing of that side of reading

which is really hard study, an effort of
duty, matter of meditation and reveren-
tial thought. I need speak not of such
reading as that of the Bible; the moral
reflections of Socrates, of Aristotle, of
Confucius; the *Confessions* of St. Augustine and the *City of God;* the dis-
courses of St. Bernard, of Bossuet, of
Bishop Butler, of Jeremy Taylor; the
vast philosophical visions that were
opened to the eyes of Bacon and Descartes; the thoughts of Pascal and Vau-
venargues, of Diderot and Hume, of
Condorcet and de Maistre; the problem
of man's nature as it is told in the *Ex-
cursion*, or in *Faust*, in *Cain*, or in the
Pilgrim's Progress; the unsearchable
outpouring of the heart in the great
mystics of many ages and many races;
be the mysticism that of David or of
John; of Mahomet or of Bouddha; of
Fénelon or of Shelley; of à Kempis or
of Goethe.

I pass by all these. For I am speaking now of the use of books in our leisure hours. I will take the books of simple enjoyment, books that one can laugh over and weep over; and learn from, and laugh or weep again; which have in them humour, truth, human nature in all its sides, pictures of the great phases of human history ; and withal sound teaching in honesty, manliness, gentleness, patience. Of such books, I say, books accepted by the voice of all mankind as matchless and immortal, there is a complete library at hand for every man, in his every mood, whatever his tastes or his acquirements. To know merely the hundred volumes or so of which I have spoken would involve the study of years. But who can say that these books are read as they might be, that we do not neglect them for something in a new cover, or which catches our eye in a library ? It is not merely to

the idle and unreading world that this
complaint holds good. It is the insatiable readers themselves who so often read
to the least profit. Of course they have
read all these household books many
years ago, read them, and judged them,
and put them away for ever. They will
read infinite dissertations about these
authors ; they will write you essays on
their works ; they will talk most learned
criticism about them. But it never
occurs to them that such books have a
daily and perpetual value, such as the
devout Christian finds in his morning
and evening psalm; that the music of
them has to sink into the soul by continual renewal ; that we have to live
with them and in them, till their ideal
world habitually surrounds us in the
midst of the real world ; that their great
thoughts have to stir us daily anew, and
their generous passion has to warm us
hour by hour ; just as we need each day

to have our eyes filled by the light of
heaven, and our blood warmed by the
glow of the sun. I vow that, when I see
men, forgetful of the perennial poetry
of the world, muckraking in a litter of
fugitive refuse, I think of that wonderful scene in the *Pilgrim's Progress*,
where the Interpreter shows the wayfarers the old man raking in the straw
and dust, whilst he will not see the
Angel who offers him a crown of gold
and precious stones.

This gold, refined beyond the standard
of the goldsmith, these pearls of great
price, the united voice of mankind has
assured us are found in those immortal
works of every age and of every race
whose names are household words
throughout the world. And we shut
our eyes to them for the sake of the
straw and litter of the nearest library
or bookshop. A lifetime will hardly
suffice to know, as they ought to be

known, these great masterpieces of man's genius. How many of us can name ten men who may be said entirely to know (in the sense in which a thoughtful Christian knows the Psalms and the Epistles) even a few of the greatest? I take them almost at random, and I name Homer, Æschylus, Aristophanes, Virgil, Dante, Ariosto, Shakespeare, Cervantes, Calderon, Corneille, Molière, Milton, Fielding, Goethe, Scott. Of course every one has read these, but who really knows them, the whole meaning of them? They are too often taken "as read," as they say in the railway meetings.

Take of this immortal choir the liveliest, the easiest, the most familiar, take for the moment the three—Cervantes, Molière, Fielding. Here we have three men who unite the profoundest insight into human nature with the most inimitable wit: *Penseroso* and *L'Allegro* in

one; "sober, steadfast, and demure,"
and yet with "Laughter holding both
his sides." And in all three, different
as they are, is an unfathomable pathos,
a brotherly pity for all human weakness,
spontaneous sympathy with all human
goodness. To know *Don Quixote*, that
is to follow out the whole mystery of its
double world, is to know the very tragi-
comedy of human life, the contrast of
the ideal with the real, of chivalry with
good sense, of heroic failure with vulgar
utility, of the past with the present, of
the impossible sublime with the possible
commonplace. And yet to how many
reading men is *Don Quixote* little more
than a book to laugh over in boyhood!
So Molière is read or witnessed; we
laugh and we praise. But how little do
we study with insight that elaborate
gallery of human character; those consummate types of almost every social
phenomenon; that genial and just judge

of imposture, folly, vanity, affectation, and insincerity ; that tragic picture of the brave man born out of his time, too proud and too just to be of use in his age ! Was ever truer word said than that about Fielding as "the prose Homer of human nature"?   And yet how often do we forget in *Tom Jones* the beauty of unselfishness, the well-spring of goodness, the tenderness, the manly healthiness and heartiness underlying its frolic and its satire, because we are absorbed, it may be, in laughing at its humour, or are simply irritated by its grossness ! Nay, *Robinson Crusoe* contains (not for boys but for men) more religion, more philosophy, more psychology, more political economy, more anthropology, than are found in many elaborate treatises on these special subjects.   And yet, I imagine, grown men do not often read *Robinson Crusoe*, as the article has it, " for instruction of life and ensample of manners." The great books of the world we have once read; we take them as read; we believe that we read them; at least, we believe that we know them. But to how few of us are they the daily mental food! For once that we take down our Milton, and read a book of that "voice," as Wordsworth says, "whose sound is like the sea," we take up fifty times a magazine with something about Milton, or about Milton's grandmother, or a book stuffed with curious facts about the houses in which he lived, and the juvenile ailments of his first wife.

And whilst the roll of the great men yet unread is to all of us so long, whilst years are not enough to master the very least of them, we are incessantly searching the earth for something new or strangely forgotten. Brilliant essays are for ever extolling some minor light. It becomes the fashion to grow rapturous

about the obscure Elizabethan dramatists; about the note of refinement in
the lesser men of Queen Anne; it is
pretty to swear by Lyly's *Euphues* and
Sidney's *Arcadia;* to vaunt Lovelace
and Herrick, Marvell and Donne, Robert
Burton and Sir Thomas Browne. All of
them are excellent men, who have written
delightful things, that may very well be
enjoyed when we have utterly exhausted
the best. But when one meets bevies of
hyper-æsthetic young maidens, in lack-a-
daisical gowns, who simper about Greene
and John Ford (authors, let us trust,
that they never have read) one wonders
if they all know *Lear* or ever heard of
Alceste. Since to nine out of ten of the
" general readers," the very best is as
yet more than they have managed to
assimilate, this fidgeting after something
curious is a little premature and perhaps
artificial.

For this reason I stand amazed at the

lengths of fantastic curiosity to which
persons, far from learned, have pushed
the mania for collecting rare books, or
prying into out-of the-way holes and cor-
ners of literature. They conduct themselves as if all the works attainable
by ordinary diligence were to them
sucked as dry as an orange. Says one,
"I came across a very curious book,
mentioned in a parenthesis in the *Religio
Medici:* only one other copy exists in
this country." I will not mention the
work, because I know that, if I did, at
least fifty libraries would be ransacked
for it, which would be unpardonable
waste of time. "I am bringing out,"
says another quite simply, "the lives of
the washerwomen of the Queens of England."   And when it comes out we shall
have a copious collection of washing-
books some centuries old, and at length
understand the mode of ironing a ruff
in the early mediæval period. A very

learned friend of mine thinks it perfectly monstrous that a public library
should be without an adequate collection
of works in Dutch, though I believe he
is the only frequenter of it who can read
that language. Not long ago I procured
for a Russian scholar a manuscript copy
of a very rare work by Greene, the contemporary of Shakespeare. Greene's
Funeralls is, I think, as dismal and
worthless a set of lines as one often sees ;
and as it has slumbered for nearly three
hundred years, I should be willing to let
it be its own undertaker. But this un-
savoury carrion is at last to be dug out
of its grave ; for it is now translated
into Russian and published in Moscow (to
the honour and glory of the Russian professor) in order to delight and inform the
Muscovite public, where perhaps not ten
in a million can as much as read Shakespeare. This or that collector again,
with the labour of half a lifetime and

by means of half his fortune, has amassed
a library of old plays, every one of them
worthless in diction, in plot, in sentiment, and in purpose ; a collection far
more stupid and uninteresting in fact
than the burlesques and pantomimes of
the last fifty years. And yet this insatiable student of old plays will probably
know less of Molière and Alfieri than
Molière's housekeeper or Alfieri's valet ;
and possibly he has never looked into
such poets as Calderon and Lope de
Vega.

Collecting rare books and forgotten
authors is perhaps of all the collecting
manias the most foolish in our day.
There is much to be said for rare china
and curious beetles. The china is occa-
sionally beautiful ; and the beetles at
least are droll. But rare books now are,
by the nature of the case, worthless
books; and their rarity usually consists
in this, that the printer made a blunder

in the text, or that they contain something exceptionally nasty or silly. To
affect a profound interest in neglected
authors and uncommon books, is a sign
for the most part—not that a man has
exhausted the resources of ordinary literature—but that he has no real respect
for the greatest productions of the greatest men of the world. This bibliomania
seizes hold of rational beings and so
perverts them, that in the sufferer's
mind the human race exists for the sake
of the books, and not the books for the
sake of the human race. There is one
book they might read to good purpose,
the doings of a great book collector—
who once lived in La Mancha. To the
collector, and sometimes to the scholar,
the book becomes a fetich or idol, and is
worthy of the worship of mankind, even
if it be not of the slightest use to any-
body. As the book exists, it must have
the compliment paid it of being invited

to the shelves. The "library is imperfect without it," although the library will, so to speak, stink when it is there. The great books are of course the common books; and these are treated by collectors and librarians with sovereign contempt. The more dreadful an abortion of a book the rare volume may be, the more desperate is the struggle of libraries to possess it. Civilisation in fact has evolved a complete apparatus, an order of men, and a code of ideas, for the express purpose one may say of degrading the great books. It suffocates them under mountains of little books, and gives the place of honour to that which is plainly literary carrion.

Now I suppose, at the bottom of all this lies that rattle and restlessness of life which belongs to the industrial Maelström wherein we ever revolve. And connected therewith comes also that literary dandyism, which results from the pursuit of letters without any social purpose or any systematic faith. To read from the pricking of some cerebral itch rather than from a desire of forming judgments ; to get, like an Alpine club stripling, to the top of some unscaled pinnacle of culture ; to use books as a sedative, as a means of exciting a mild intellectual titillation, instead of as a means of elevating the nature ; to dribble on in a perpetual literary gossip, in order to avoid the effort of bracing the mind to think—such is our habit in an age of utterly chaotic education. We read, as the bereaved poet made rhymes—

"For the unquiet heart and brain,
A use in measured language lies;
The sad mechanic exercise,
Like dull narcotics, numbing pain."

We, to whom steam and electricity have given almost everything excepting bigger

brains and hearts, who have a new invention ready for every meeting of the
Royal Institution, who want new things
to talk about faster than children want
new toys to break, we cannot take up
the books we have seen about us since
our childhood: Milton, or Molière, or
Scott. It feels like donning knee-
breeches and buckles, to read what
everybody has read, what everybody
can read, and which our very fathers
thought good entertainment scores of
years ago. Hard-worked men and over-
wrought women crave an occupation
which shall free them from their
thoughts and yet not take them from
their world. And thus it comes that
we need at least a thousand new books
every season, whilst we have rarely a
spare hour left for the greatest of all.
But I am getting into a vein too serious
for our purpose: education is a long
and thorny topic. I will cite but the

words on this head of the great Bishop Butler. " The great number of books and papers of amusement which, of one kind or another, daily come in one's way, have in part occasioned, and most perfectly fall in with and humour, this idle way of reading and considering things. By this means time, even in solitude, is happily got rid of, without the pain of attention ; neither is any part of it more put to the account of idleness, one can scarce forbear saying is spent with less thought, than great part of that which is spent in reading." But this was written a century and a half ago, in 1729 ; since which date, let us trust, the multiplicity of print and the habits of desultory reading have considerably abated.

A philosopher with whom I hold (but whose opinions I have no present intention of propounding) proposed a method of dealing with this indiscriminate use of books, which I think is worthy of attention. He framed a short collection of books for constant and general reading. He put it forward " with the view of guiding the more thoughtful minds among the people in their choice for constant use." He declares that " both the intellect and the moral character suffer grievously at the present time from irregular reading." It was not intended to put a bar upon other reading, or to supersede special study. It is designed as a type of a healthy and rational syllabus of essential books, fit for common teaching and daily use. It presents a working epitome of what is best and most enduring in the literature of the world. The entire collection would form in the shape in which books now exist in modern libraries, something like five hundred volumes. They embrace books both of ancient and modern times, in all the five principal languages of modern Europe.   It is divided into four sections : Poetry, Science, History, Religion.

The principles on what it is framed are these : First, it collects the best in all the great departments of human thought, so that no part of education shall be wholly wanting.   Next, it puts together the greatest books, of universal and permanent value, and the greatest and the most enduring only.   Next, it measures the greatness of books not by their brilliancy, or even their learning, but by their power of presenting some typical chapter in thought, some dominant phase of history; or else it measures them by their power of idealising man and nature, or of giving harmony to our moral and intellectual activity. Lastly, the test of the general value of books is the permanent relation they bear to the common civilisation of Europe.

Some such firm foot-hold in the vast
and increasing torrent of literature it is
certainly urgent to find, unless all that
is great in literature is to be borne away
in the flood of books. With this, we
may avoid an interminable wandering
over a pathless waste of waters. Without it, we may read everything and know
nothing ; we may be curious about anything that chances, and indifferent to
everything that profits. Having such a
catalogue before our eyes, with its perpetual warning—*non multa sed multum*
—we shall see how with our insatiable
consumption of print we wander, like
unclassed spirits, round the outskirts
only of those Elysian fields where the
great dead dwell and hold high converse.
As it is we hear but in a faint echo that
voice which cries :—

"Onorate l'altissimo Poeta:
 L'ombra sua torna, ch'era dipartita."

We need to be reminded every day, how many are the books of inimitable glory, which, with all our eagerness after reading, we have never taken in our hands. It will astonish most of us to find how much of our very industry is given to the books which leave no mark, how often we rake in the litter of the printing-press, whilst a crown of gold and rubies is offered us in vain.

POSTSCRIPT.—I have elsewhere given, with some explanation and introduction, the library of Auguste Comte, which forms the basis of the whole of the essay above. The catalogue is to be found in many of his publications, as the *Catechism*, Trübner and Co. (translated : London, 1858); and also in the fourth volume of the *Positive Polity* (translated: London, 1877, pp. 362, 483), where its use and meaning are explained. Those who may take an erroneous idea of its purpose, and may think that such a catalogue would serve in the

way of an ordinary circulating library,
may need to be reminded that it is designed
as the basis of a scheme of education, for
one particular system of philosophy, and
as the manual of an organised form of religion.   It is, in fact, the literary resumé
of Positivist teaching ; and as such alone
can it be used.   It is, moreover, designed
to be of common use to all Western Europe,
and to be ultimately extended to all classes.
It is essentially a people's library for popular instruction; it is of permanent use
only; and it is intended to serve as a type.
Taken in connection with the *Calendar*,
which contains the names of nearly two
hundred and fifty authors, it may serve as
a guide of the books "that the world
would not willingly let die."   But it must
be remembered that it has no special relation to current views of education, to English literature, much less to the literature
of the day.   It was drawn up thirty years
ago by a French philosopher, who passed
his life in Paris, and who had read no new

books for twenty years. And it was de-
signedly limited by him to such a compass
that hard-worked men might hope to
master it; in order to give them an *aperçu*
of what the ancient and the modern world
had left of most great in each language
and in each department of thought. To
attempt to use it, or to judge it, from any
point of view but this, would be entirely to
mistake its character and object.

THE WORKS OF
WILLIAM WINTER.

SHAKESPEARE'S ENGLAND. 18MO, CLOTH, 75 CENTS.

GRAY DAYS AND GOLD. 18MO, CLOTH, 75 CENTS.

SHADOWS OF THE STAGE. 18MO, CLOTH, 75 CENTS.

OLD SHRINES AND IVY. 18MO, CLOTH, 75 CENTS.

Also a Small Limited LARGE PAPER EDITION. 4 Vols. Uniform. $8.00.

WANDERERS: A Collection of Poems. NEW EDITION. WITH A PORTRAIT. 18MO, CLOTH, 75 CENTS.

"The supreme need of this age in America is a practical conviction that progress does not consist in material prosperity, but in spiritual advancement. Utility has long been exclusively worshipped. The welfare of the future lies in the worship of beauty. To that worship these pages are devoted, with all that implies of sympathy with the higher instincts, and faith in the divine destiny of the human race."—*From the Preface to Gray Days and Gold.*

MACMILLAN & CO.,
NEW YORK.

www.ingramcontent.com/pod-product-compliance
Lightning Source LLC
Chambersburg PA
CBHW020231030726
47497CB00009B/3050